BOOK TEN OF THE GIFTED WORLD SERIES

THE FINAL FALLOUT

L. D. VALENCIA

THE FINAL FALLOUT

Book 10

L. D. Valencia

Dedicated to Chris Chicago. A brother taken too soon.

CONTENTS

PROLOGUE

"About time, Snakes." Marcus Pharis had been standing in the dark building for an hour, waiting for his associate to arrive.

"Please express my deepest sympathies to the Oculus," said the associate, his voice sounding almost snake-like.

"Do you have the diamonds?" Pharis asked.

"Yes," said the associate. "Here are your diamonds."

He handed him a large black pouch. Pharis put his hand in, pulling out several small diamonds. He looked up. "Here is the venisium."

Marcus held up a metal briefcase. Inside was a piece of a shimmering green gemstone. The man, known as Snakes, pulled the gemstone out and studied it. Just by holding it, he could feel the power inside of him rising and increasing to an impossible degree. He nodded and looked back at Marcus. "Well, this is some impressive stuff, isn't it?"

"It's the real thing."

"Good. My organization thanks you," said Snakes.

"Good, so we have a deal?" Pharis raised an eyebrow.

"Yes."

"Well, where's my extra ten percent?" Marcus asked, rubbing his reddish beard.

"I only have five percent. Things are, uh, tight, you know."

"The deal was ten percent. I'm giving you first dibs on the last source of venisium in the world. This is the only venisium you are going to get, and now you tell me you can't give me what we agreed upon?" Marcus said.

"Listen, Marcus, you know me. We're buddies." He fought the urge to take a step back.

"Hardly. We are business associates. Nothing more."

Snake placed a hand over his heart, his face twisting into a mock wounded expression. "You wound me, Marcus. How about this? I go back to the boss man and I tell him that we will get you the other five percent. How about that?"

"I don't think so, Snakes. Deal's off." He tossed the bag of diamonds at Snakes' feet and then turned to grab the venisium briefcase.

But Snakes had other plans. He turned around and engaged his gift. Two large tendrils of energy sprang from his hands like twin cobras. He threw the first energy whip at Marcus. The energy ripped through the man's shirt, cutting off his shirt sleeve and exposing a long, red gash.

Pharis chuckled. "That was unwise."

But Snakes didn't let up. He swung again, but this time Pharis caught the energy whip. He then engaged his own gift. Snakes felt a strange fatigue wash over him. It was almost like he became impossibly tired for no reason whatsoever. Immediately, he dropped to his knees. The energy whips faded into nothing.

Marcus looked down at him as he put his foot on his chest and then kicked him back onto the ground. "Consider this a personal courtesy. Normally, I would kill someone for what you just did. But I don't need a blood war on my hands. So, you get to live. Next time you or anyone in your organization comes anywhere near me, I won't be so kind. Understand me?"

Snakes nodded slowly.

"Good, thank you," he said. "I will be billing you for the suit. This shirt was made of Mulberry silk."

Pharis grabbed the bag of diamonds and tossed it in the air a few times before pulling out a small handful of diamonds. "Consider this payment for the shirt."

Then he turned away and walked down the long, dark stairwell to the exit. Outside, a car filled with guards and support crew was waiting. He got into the car and sprawled out on the black leather. His assistant looked up as he sat in the backseat, but then looked back down at her tablet. A quarter of a second later, she looked up again, her eyes wide.

"Sir, what happened?" she asked, concerned.

"The Death-Tone Gang is out. Who's our next buyer?" asked Marcus.

"That would be the Octavians," she said.

"Have you confirmed their price?" Marcus asked.

"Yes, they are willing to pay the extra ten percent."

"I hope so," said Pharis. "The Death-Tones didn't seem so willing once it was time to pay up."

"Shall we head that way, sir?" asked the assistant.

"Yes, call them now and tell them we are on our way."

"Very good," she said.

THE BREAKOUT

"Red alert!" The siren's robotic voice filled the hallways.

Sentry looked over at his best friend and partner, Brimstone. They shared a split-second look and then ran to the exit. Together they ran down the stairs and to the main hallway. Several other agents were gathering outside of the War Room.

"What's going on?" asked Sentry.

Foundry looked over to them. "Looks like we have a situation on our hands. A crime syndicate called the Octavians are attacking a gifted prison installation on the outskirts of the state. We're prepping and sending out teams as we speak."

Captain V, one of the five leaders of the Guild Agency, was grouping up agents and sending them into the teleportation hub. "You four, go now."

Sentry and Brimstone looked at each other and pushed forward. The crush of agents was starting to thin out, and they made their way to the front. Foundry had been paired with another group. It made sense, she was one of the best Tanks they had in the entire agency. Then it was their turn.

"All right," said V. "You two pair up with Agent Nash and Agent Penta. I want Sentry on defense, while you three keep up a ranged attack. We have reports that the Octavian crime syndicate is trying to blast their way into the prison."

"Do we know what they're after?" asked Sentry.

"The head of the crime family is in custody there. My guess is that they're breaking her out," said V.

"That's insane. They don't have a chance," said Brimstone.

"I don't know. They must have a trick up their sleeves if they are actually trying to break her out. How else can you explain an insane attack like this? Now, hurry!"

Then he turned and pushed them through the door. Immediately, a teleporter in the next room was waving them over. She sent them through a blue-green portal. They came through on the other side to something akin to a war zone. Explosions could be heard in the distance. From their vantage point, they could see the prison three or four hundred yards to their left. Just beyond that was a cliff face and then the ocean.

Now that he had scanned the area, Sentry quickly produced a shield to protect his teammates. Behind him, Nash and Penta were both powering up their gifts. Brimstone was beside Sentry, a flame already dancing in his hand. He tapped Sentry on the back and they moved together. Brimstone kept his arm on Sentry's back as if to guide him. The other two maintained a perimeter, but they were still close enough to be in the shielded area.

The first contacts they made were a group of blasters that were firing on the prison walls. The walls were massive and should have been all but impenetrable. The damage they were doing to the wall was impressive, but fortunately, Sentry and his team were able to get the drop on them since their attention was on the wall. Brimstone lobbed a fireball at them that sent them all flying while Nash picked off anyone who was still conscious with a sonic blast. Penta had the most range on her blasts, so she fired at the next group, picking them off from almost one hundred yards off.

"Nice work, team!" yelled Brimstone.

They pushed on to see another group targeting the wall and rushed forward, still maintaining their tight formation. Nash hit them with a sonic burst that dropped them all to their knees. Then

Penta picked them off with targeted shots that knocked them all out. When they approached the area the group had been blasting, Sentry noticed something—a crystal—on the ground.

"What's that?" Brimstone asked, walking over.

Sentry picked it up and realized what it was. The small glowing stone wasn't a crystal. It was venisium. Flashbacks to the fight with Quiet—a fight he would remember for the rest of his life—spun through his mind. The warlike struggle, the explosions...Then he realized where he was.

"This is venisium!" Sentry called out.

"What?" Brimstone tilted his head and crossed his arms. "How's that possible?"

"I don't know," said Sentry. "We collected the venisium and sent it to the Protectorate."

"How did they get it?" Brimstone tapped his foot impatiently, eager to move.

"I don't know, but we need to get moving. If these people have venisium, we have our work cut out for us."

The team moved through the Octavian blasters, taking on the groups they encountered. Fortunately, they didn't find any more members that had those venisium stones. The number of gang members was more concentrated closer to the wall, and the fighting was more intense. A row of guards was trying to hold the line against the Octavian gang members. They also had some on top of the wall, blasting down on them as well, but that didn't seem to be stopping them. As they approached, Sentry could see that one of the Octavians was projecting a massive force field that deflected all of the blasts from above and below.

"How is that shield holding?" asked Nash.

"I don't know," said Sentry. "It's getting hit from all over."

"What do we do?" asked Nash.

"We take it down!" said Sentry.

They moved in that direction with Penta firing from a distance. They hit a few other random groups of Octavians here and there while making their way to the force field, but Sentry had little trouble keeping them shielded. His confidence grew with each takedown. It was a strange surge of energy, having this new power. He found himself liking it.

Most of the Octavian's attention was focused on the wall, which was now looking like it would collapse. Then, when they were fired on, he was able to easily deflect the blasts. As they approached, they found another group of agents.

"About time you got here," said Granite.

"I thought I could hear the sound of someone eating rocks," said Brimstone.

Granite laughed. "Nice one."

"How do we get inside that force field?" asked Penta.

Granite and his team looked stumped. "If I knew, I would already be inside," Granite said. "We've been hitting it from here since the moment we got here. But we haven't been able to crack this one."

"What if we went under it?" asked Sentry.

"Under it?" Granite snapped his fingers. "Why didn't I think of that?"

Granite and Sentry got their teams set. Then Granite used his terrakinetic gift to open a massive hole in the ground. Several of the agents were able to travel down into the tunnel, where they were then able to invade the force field. Sentry was the first one inside and pushed forward as the tank. He shielded himself as the Octavian blasters fired at him. Granite, who was right behind him, held out his hand and summoned rock walls in between them and the Octavians and then broke them off. Debris rained down on their enemies. Several of them found themselves trapped in a rocky tomb.

That leveled the playing field a little, but the real problem was the force field. Sentry needed to find whoever was creating it so they could shut it down. He risked a backwards glance to make sure his team was still with him. Nash was moving to the left, away from the group. Sentry opened his mouth to ask Nash what was going on when an explosion rocked his world. Dirt went flying everywhere, and Nash was gone.

Sentry's eyes widened. "We need to find that force field, now."

"I think I see her…"

Sentry's heart dropped into his stomach. Penta had near-perfect vision. If she couldn't see the missing agent, one could only assume the worst.

She pointed toward the center of the area. A woman was holding her hands out. Around her was a bubble deflecting all kinds of explosions and energy blasts. A bright green glow emanated from one of her palms. There was no doubt about it. She was using venisium. It was augmenting her gifts to an almost-godlike level.

"We need to team up and hit her with everything we have at once," said Sentry.

Granite was frozen in place. Something was getting to him. Sentry put a hand on his shoulder. Granite shook his head, trying to snap himself out of it. He couldn't think about what happened the last time they got into a fight with someone who had venisium. He couldn't think about Zion.

"Everyone swarm in now!"

Sentry and Granite moved first, holding the line for the blasters to attack. Penta was probably their heaviest hitter, so again and again, she launched blasts of energy at the force field, but nothing seemed to penetrate the shield.

Sentry and Granite both slammed into the shield. Energy crackled as they collided with the force field. There was a loud hissing sound, followed by the pungent smell of burning. Sentry pushed further, trying with everything he had. When his shield collided with the force field, he felt it give way. But the force field didn't break. The woman looked at them with a smile. It was obvious she had no concern for them at all. Turning, she returned her attention to the wall.

"This isn't working," yelled Granite.

"Try to shift the ground," he yelled back.

Granite nodded. "I will do you one better."

The earth began to rumble, rolling like a wave, until water and dirt shot up from underneath the enemy's feet and she was sent flying up into the air. There was a break in her concentration and the shield dissolved. Sentry pulled at the stone while Granite surrounded both of her arms with rocks and pinned her down. While she was dazed, Sentry managed to rip the stone from her grasp. Once she realized what had happened, she thrashed and kicked at the air.

"Read her rights." Sentry looked over at the wall, which was all but broken. Somehow, they had held off the attack. If they hadn't taken the force field user down, they would have been through it soon. They had just barely handled this mission.

With the exception of those that had run away, the Octavians were brought in and captured. After the area was secured, Sentry met with V and Captain Ein, still holding the piece of venisium aloft with his telekinesis. He was afraid to even touch it, in case it could be used as evidence. When V saw the stone floating there, his eyes widened as he covered his mouth in disbelief.

"How is this possible?" asked Sentry. "I thought we gave the last of the venisium to the Protectorate."

Captain V was staring at it as if he was waiting for the shard to explode at any moment. "We did. Unless there's more of it somewhere else. But that can't be. All of the venisium has been accounted for, but this isn't synthetic. This is the real deal."

"Regardless of how this got into their hands, nice work," Ein said. "You are to be commended."

"We were lucky. If we hadn't been able to get the drop of them, we would have been dealing with a much different situation here," Sentry said.

"I think this is just the beginning. I think we may be dealing with a whole new problem," said V.

FILE #2

TWO WEEKS EARLIER

The entire entourage of agents appeared in the teleportation zone. Agent Fault stood at the center, surrounded by the entire team. The case containing the venisium was still attached to her hand. Behind her stood one of the legends of the Protectorate—and by far, the oldest living person in the world. Director Zeno.

As they exited the teleportation zone, she thought to herself, *What king of stories must he have?*

Every ounce of her wanted to ask him about the things he must have seen, the adventures he had in his time. But she was on duty. She couldn't look unprofessional, especially not in front of Zeno. He was the director of the Protectorate Academy. He knew everyone and worked with the best agents in the world. Part of her wondered if she looked good in front of him and maybe she could strike up the courage to speak with him. But first, she needed to deliver the venisium.

The entire team marched down the hall. A surge of pride welled up inside her as they passed the other agents and employees. She wondered what they all thought of her. Although she wasn't the ones who had acquired this venisium, she liked to think that the other agents would believe she was. Maybe they thought of her as one of those field agents who had been there in Turkey. She'd heard the story. An agent named Sentry and a team from the Guild were the ones who had stopped a terrorist group. Apparently the enemy had been a former agent named Quiet. To think someone could turn so far off course.

Not like Director Zeno. He was one of the most well-respected individuals in the entire Protectorate. He was the kind of person that everyone wanted to work for and everyone wished they could be.

A team of guards stood in front of a large metallic door with a massive lock one it. It looked like the type you might find deep inside the most impressive bank.

"Report?" asked the first guard.

"We have a case of very sensitive material." He handed the first guard a form.

The guard took the form and put it in the filing box at the front. "All right, you all are cleared." The guard's demeanor changed once he realized that Director Zeno was standing among the agents and he started nodding, almost subconsciously. "Please, follow me."

He walked them to the door, even though it wasn't necessary since they were standing directly in front of it. He pressed his hand to the door and the scanner soundlessly sprang to life and read his palm. The device also required a code, which the guard promptly punched into the touch screen. After imputing each number, he looked over his shoulder to see if Zeno was watching him. Then the gate opened in front of them, and the guard held out a hand for them to enter.

He watched Zeno as all of the other agents walked inside of the vault. "H-have a nice day, Director Zeno."

Bartholomew Zeno nodded. "Thank you."

Inside the vault, they found a room with multiple layers of metal along the walls. Agent Fault noticed the bolts running up and down the metallic plating. Ahead she could see a massive system of lockers and drawers like inside a bank. There were guards posted at every corner, along with a small team at the center.

Another team of guards took the case from Fault while Agent Silver looked over the exchange. A large woman approached in full tactical gear.

"That will be all. You and your team are relieved. But we thank you for your service."

Fault and Silver, along with the rest of the team, nodded. They were slowly checked out by the previous guard team as they left. The star struck guard once again approached Director Zeno. "Sir, can I get you anything?"

"Oh no, thank you. I will be heading back to the Academy now."

The guard nodded. "Very good, sir."

The rest of the team counted each guard, making sure everyone was accounted for. Zeno nodded at Fault in the hallway. "Well, I appreciate all of your work, team. I guess this is where we part ways."

He turned and walked in the opposite, whistling as he left.

"Sir, the exit is this way."

"Oh, I'm going to take the long way around. I'd like to speak with some of the team members here."

No one spoke as he continued walking off. The entire crew of agents watched in varying degrees of shock and awe. Fault was the most impressed of them all. She wished she had a reason to follow him. She was supposed to report back immediately, but she lingered, watching him until he rounded the corner out of sight. With a sigh, she turned and left.

Down the hall, Director Zeno was nodding his head as he passed a group of staffers gathered around a coffee machine. "Well, what's the latest on the floor?"

Two of the staffers recognized him from his last visit, while the rest only knew him by name. "Director Zeno, it's nice to see you again," said one of the staffers.

"How are things at the U.S. academy?" asked the other.

The rest gave warm welcomes. "We were just discussing the Quiet case."

"Ah yes," said Director Zeno. "Terrible situation, indeed. I can't believe someone would do something like that and betray the Protectorate."

Inside, Zeno was smiling, however, on the outside, he put on a sad, stoic expression. He looked far off for a moment to really sell the lie. Then he made a fist and pounded his other hand. "We will make sure those who work against the Protectorate and work to harm others are caught."

The group of staffers all nodded and a few even cheered as he spoke. This particular group of staffers were on a topic he didn't want to pursue too much further. In his experience, he got the most information when he approached a group that were talking about a topic that he wanted to know more about. If he forced them to change topics, the conversation never seemed to garner quite as much information, so Zeno nodded to them all and looked down the hall.

"Well, everyone, remember you are the backbone of our organization. Thank you for your work," he said. Then he turned and headed down the hall. As he walked, he shook the hands of several of the personal assistants. If he wasn't mistaken, this next wing was the South American branch. He needed to see if there were any developments on the Velasquez case so he sidled up beside the staffers as they were working.

"We still haven't located the source of his suppliers," he heard one of them say.

Inside, Bartholomew smiled. *Good, they still haven't tracked down my sources.* Then he leaned in and said to the staffers, "Have you thought about planting a mole in his organization?"

"We've thought about it, but this cartel doesn't use anyone that isn't family," said the staffer as he looked up. Once he realized it was Bartholomew Zeno and not just a regular staffer, he dropped his pen and stood at attention. "Sir, I didn't realize it was you."

"No problem, son. I was just offering up an idea," Zeno said with a smile.

"How do you know about the Velasquez case, sir?" asked another staffer.

With a laugh, Zeno answered, "I know about more cases than you know about, young lady. I have been around here longer than the dirt in the flower beds outside."

The staffers responded with a mix of laughs and fake smiles. Many were in genuine awe of Zeno, but a few were too nervous to be themselves. Zeno rubbed elbows with the staffers for several more minutes. After he was certain they were on the wrong trail, he decided to leave.

"Well, I feel you're all on the right path, so I'll leave you all to it. Best of luck on the case."

He walked toward the main escalators that led to the exit. Immediately after he reached the ground floor, a small troop of agents cut him off from his escape. He tilted his head slightly as the lead agent spoke.

"Sir, there is a situation. We need you to come with us."

"What seems to be the problem," Zeno asked, doing his best to sound uncertain.

The entire team of agents looked at each other, sharing an uncomfortable look. The one just behind the lead agent turned back to Zeno. "Sir, we will have to discuss that in private. Will you please come with us?"

Zeno nodded and they escorted him to one of the elevators, where they rode down in silence. Zeno knew they were returning to the vault, but he retained that mask of confusion. As a practiced liar, he was sure that he could keep up this deception with no issue at all. Finally, they hit the bottom floor and the elevator opened. In front of them, he saw several agents as well as an important individual.

"Director Zeno," said Lady Frey, Head of the Protectorate. "Will you please come this way?"

"Of course," he said, stepping out of the elevator. "What seems to be the situation?"

"Once we placed the venisium stones into the vault, we had our team begin cataloging them. However, when they did so, they realized something."

"What was that?" Zeno asked, feigning shock.

"Several of the stones were missing."

Zeno's eyes widened. He looked around for a moment and then back to Lady Frey. "Where could they have gone?" he asked. "They were inspected before we left Turkey."

"Exactly. So, either someone inside of the Protectorate building got to them, or they were taken before you even arrived," said Lady Frey.

"Well, what do we need to do?"

A tinge of red touched her cheeks. "Well, we actually need to scan you to make sure you don't have them."

"Me," he said, somewhat indignantly. He stood there for a moment and then nodded. "I understand. No one is above the law. We have to inspect every possible angle."

He walked over to her as one of her agents approached from behind. The agent waved her hand up and down in front of him. Her eyes changed to a glassy gray color. Then she dropped her hand and looked to Frey. "He doesn't have them on him."

"Very good. I am relieved to hear that, although I wasn't too worried," she said with a false smile.

"Neither was I," said Zeno. "But who knows who could be working against us. It is possible someone could have planted them on me."

"I suppose so."

"However, we are still left wondering what happened. I supposed we have only one other alternative for our culprits then."

"What do you mean?" she asked.

"The only people to have access to those stones were your agents, myself, and the agent from the Guild. It must have been one of them. I think we need to bring each of those agents in."

She looked concerned for a moment. Then she nodded. "I will send a team to investigate it immediately."

As he was escorted out of the room, Zeno had a devilish grin on his face that lasted until he exited the building. He walked down the main stone walkway and to the large black car that was waiting for him. His personal driver was waiting for him. He opened the door for Zeno, who got into the back seat, and then he sat in the front seat. "Where to, sir?"

Zeno look at the passenger in the seat opposite him. "Where should we go, Lift?"

"Wherever we can talk about our payment."

"Let's head to the base."

The driver turned onto the main road and they were off. Zeno sat in silence, looking out the window, while they drove, never giving the young lady so much as a glance. This was intentional more so than anything. Zeno knew how to play on someone's emotions. He had been doing it for years as the Director of the Protectorate Academy. He worked cadets over by making them feel inadequate. Then once he had them in his grasp, he would dangle some kind of hope in front of them. By that point, he usually had them. He could make them do whatever he wanted.

Out of the corner of his eye, he could see Lift shifting every now and then. The awkward silence was working. At this point, the young lady was probably feeling like she had no power in this situation. Which was true. But he wanted her to know it long before they made the deal.

Zeno's driver knew the protocol. It was always possible that they were followed, so the driver would take a seemingly random, scenic route. Finally, they turned off onto an abandoned road. Ahead of them was an old steel mill that was no longer in use. It used much of the old technology, so it wasn't fit to be used today. It still had massive smoke stacks and pollution causing machines. Zeno mocked the old ways of doing things in his head. The car stopped and the driver came around to let Zeno and his guest out.

"This way," Zeno said.

Zeno looked over his shoulder to see Lift looking around at the strange scene. Foreign machines still littered the open area. Broken down, shabby buildings dotted the work yard. They approached the largest building in the area, and Zeno paused before going inside. He knew at this point Lift was wondering what would happen next.

The driver opened the door for them. Inside, the building was much of what you'd expect from a rundown building. Dusty floors, a caved-in ceiling, and wires were strewn about the room. Zeno stopped in the center of the large room. "Well, here we won't be disturbed."

"All right. Well, when do I get the money?" Lift pursed her lips.

"You should be receiving the payment shortly. May I see the stones?" Zeno asked.

She took half a step back, uncertain. Her phone dinged. She smiled down at the screen. The money transfer had been successful. Immediately, her shoulders dropped, and the tightness in her back disappeared. Then she spun her hand and the stones appeared in them.

"Fantastic. You are remarkable," said Zeno.

"I'm the best," she said.

"Well, not the best. I know the best. I have used the best. You are extraordinary indeed. Maybe a close third or fourth, if you're lucky. However, this specific situation requires no loose ends," Zeno said.

A flash of light appeared and a sizzling sound filled the air. Lift looked down at her chest and saw the hole before immediately dropping to the ground.

Zeno walked over to her and looked down at Lift's body with genuine sadness. "It's a shame, really. She did have so much potential."

"Indeed," Lightbringer said, stepping out of the shadows. "But like you said, this was a very sensitive situation. We can't afford to have any witnesses." With a flick of her wrist, a shiny, metal case appeared.

"If only situations had been different. It's a shame that things had to end up this way."

Bartholomew Zeno bent down and picked up the stones. They all gleamed with an otherworldly hue, which gave them a haunting look. He handed them to Lightbringer, who placed three stones into the small slots embedded in the case. Then she locked it and pressed the locking mechanism with her palm.

"I want to start getting these sold immediately. We can cut off shards and sell them for and impossible price. However, make sure you make it appear that the supply is incredible scarce. With these, we can name our own price."

"Very good, sir," she said. Then she paused, lingering for a moment.

Zeno took a step toward the door. Then he turned. Their business wasn't concluded just yet. He looked at her with a quizzical expression. His eyes turned to slits as he studied her demeanor. Normally, Lightbringer was all business. She was completely unflappable. Never in their time together had he seen her shaken before.

"Sir, we have another situation that demands your attention."

"What's that?" His tone was almost cavalier.

"We haven't heard from Antonia Sagas in some time now. Some Oculus members are looking for her, but we're starting to become more concerned that she may be attempting to defect."

Zeno looked up at the large hole in the ceiling. "Who do we have on this?"

"Right now, I have a team of agents working undercover in Europe. However, she could be anywhere. We don't even know where to begin."

Zeno thought for a moment. "This was a little before your time, but her parents were members in the Oculus long ago. They never were as committed to our cause. In all honesty, they were really upstanding business owners. But they did cut a few deals with us that were helpful. Nothing nefarious, mind you. Just deals on energy through their power plants."

Lightbringer didn't respond since she didn't quite understand where this was going. Zeno did this sometimes—told long stories before getting to a point. But she didn't get this high in the organization by not following orders. She was a soldier, and she followed her leader. Right now, that was Zeno.

"I always wondered if Antonia would be more malleable to our ways. It seems she isn't. Why don't you send Titus after her? He's still itching to prove himself, and this might be the perfect opportunity."

"Makes sense."

The two turned to leave and Zeno's driver opened the door for him. Zeno stepped out into the open air and popped on a pair of sunglasses as he walked to the car. Walking beside him, Lightbringer looked over. "What did the Protectorate say about the missing stones?"

"I gave them another thread to follow."

"Who?"

"I pointed them toward the Guild."

Lightbringer laughed. "Brilliant, sir."

"That reminds me. I'll need to contact one of my associates in the Protectorate. I want to make sure they put down that Agent Sentry if things get out of hand. I can't have him testifying."

"Anyone in mind?"

"I think I do."

FILE #3

SUSPECTS

Back at the Guild, Gabriel was finishing up a light workout in the training room and planned to relax in the hot tub followed by an ice bath. However, as he was heading toward the locker room, an agent came around the corner. He was one of the newer recruits, not an official field agent yet. Probably, still in that probationary period. He had a stack of forms in his hand and looked somewhat worried. He looked like at any moment he might pop like a jack-in-the-box.

"M-Mr. Sentry, sir," he stammered. "You are needed immediately."

"What's wrong?" Gabriel asked.

"There's a meeting, and I was told to bring you upstairs promptly."

"All right, let me change and I will head up in a moment."

"No, sir," said the agent. "I was told you bring you upstairs *right now*."

"Is this Protectorate business?"

The agent glanced over his shoulder. With no one in the immediate vicinity, he turned back to Gabriel and nodded. Despite the firm nod, the young man looked very uncertain about what to do next.

"Right. I'll follow you upstairs now. Wouldn't want you to get in trouble."

Gabriel followed the agent upstairs and into the War Room. Gabriel's team from the Turkish mission against Quiet—the same team he'd gone on several missions with—were sitting at the tables. At the far side was his best friend, Jake, also known as Agent Brimstone, and right next to him was Serena—Agent Insight—his former girlfriend. Near the door was Agent Codex, who was sitting next to V, who ran most of their operations. Lastly, in the far corner was Captain Ein, the head of the Guild. The different special Protectorate agents around the room, however, was somewhat odd.

But before he could count how many there were, the woman at the center of the room spoke. "About time, Agent Sentry."

She had short, spiky dark hair that matched her dark lipstick and heavy eyeshadow. Her left ear had two studs in it, but there was a large hoop earring in the right. Her arms were crossed over chest, and she looked annoyed. Her expression was stern and her body language spoke to her standing and waiting there for a long time. So, Sentry took a seat at the nearest table and folded his fingers politely.

"Well, now that everyone is here, we can begin. First off, you can call me Special Agent Brand."

"What is this about?" Captain V asked somewhat indignantly.

"We are here because of your agency's mission in Turkey two months ago. You and your team were in a war-torn country, rattled one of the most volatile and militant gift groups, and then made off with a briefcase full of venisium."

"So, we're being lectured because we conducted an operation in Turkey?" asked Ein. "My team completed their mission and made it out without drawing any attention to the Protectorate. If anything, Quiet drew their attention, and he's gone now."

"Your op was hardly clean. We're dealing with much of the fallout from that. The Protectorate is, to this day, diverting massive amounts of resources to observing and maintaining a watchful but invisible eye on the country. It is a very tenuous situation we find ourselves in."

Ein laughed. "True, Turkey's leadership is a source of tension, but it has always been that way. The Protectorate has always had to keep an eye on the Princes there."

"Yes, but—"

Ein cut her off. "My team may have attempted a risky move, but the mission was successful. We acquired the venisium and stopped it from being distributed."

Brand pursed her lips. "If only that were true. Two weeks ago, when we got the venisium from your team and brought it to the vault, there were multiple shards missing."

"What do you mean?" V raised an eyebrow. "We gave you the case."

"Yes, but once we made it to the base, there were pieces missing. It is uncertain how you or your team made off with the shards, but you're our primary suspects."

"Wait, what are you saying?" Sentry looked around at the other agents as if this was a joke he wasn't in on.

"By order of the Protectorate, you are all under arrest until we can ascertain the location of the missing shards." Brand narrowed her eyes.

"What?" Sentry's chair clattered to the floor as he abruptly stood up.

She placed her hands on her hips. "Unfortunately, these are my orders."

"Why? We completed the mission. We gave you the venisium. It isn't right."

"As it stands now, we need to bring you in so we can make sure if you were involved in the missing venisium." The special agents moved to the center of the room as she spoke and pulled out handcuffs. "Come in quietly, and we can make sure that this situation doesn't get further out of hand."

An agent clapped a pair of handcuffs onto Sentry's wrists, pressed a button in the center, and the metal clamps locked down tighter. The handcuffs were made with some kind of synthetic venisium that would dampen, if not completely nullify, a gifted's abilities. He looked down at Sentry with a cold expression that showed he had little to no remorse for what he was doing. Sentry tried to rein in his anger. He was just doing his job. But this was still unfair. It made no sense to him.

The handcuffs were made with some kind of synthetic venisium that would dampen if not completely nullify a gifted's abilities. A tingling sensation flowed up his arms and he grunted in discomfort.

Instinctively, Sentry turned to Captain V. He saw the older man standing up, with his arms out and an agent slapped handcuffs down on his wrists. V looked down at the manacles with a stoic expression. Seeing his mentor and his coach take up this mentality, Sentry turned back to the agent in front of him and stood up, looking as serious as he could manage as the agent pushed him toward the door.

Over his shoulder, Sentry could see them pushing Insight, Brimstone, and the others into the hallway. The special agents around them maintained a tight perimeter around them, either pushing or pulling them with a little more force than necessary.

Once they stepped into the main lobby, the looks they got were strange and haunting. Most of the other Guild members looked at them with a combination of shock and judgement. Even though Sentry knew they hadn't done anything wrong, it appeared they were already being judged as guilty.

He dropped his head, trying to push the thoughts away and maintain that austere expression. He wanted to be stoic and unflappable like Captain V, but the negative thoughts kept rolling through his mind. What must everyone in the Guild think of him? Would they ever look at him the same way again, or would they always wonder if he was guilty? Maybe it wouldn't matter in the end.

That thought shocked him as they pushed him down the escalator toward the exit. What if they convicted him of this crime, innocent or not? Would he spend the rest of his life in a maximum security gifted prison? Or would they force him into the black cells where some of the worst convicts lived, never to see the light of day again? So many thoughts played through his mind. So many horrible visions and questions that he thought he was going to break in that moment.

Then a different thought entered his mind...but it wasn't his own. Instinctively, he looked over his shoulder at Insight. Somehow she was overcoming the gift-dampening handcuffs. *Don't worry. Calm down and breathe.*

It's hard to focus on that when everything is happening so quickly, he answered.

Insight huffed. *You're an agent. You're supposed to be a professional. Keep it together.*

I'm trying...

She rolled her eyes. *Try harder.*

All right. He looked down somewhat dejectedly. *How's everyone else?*

Everyone else is somewhere in between freaking out and thinking we are going to be fine, so it's a little scattered. Insight shifted uncomfortably.

Think we are going to get out of this? Sentry asked.

It's hard to say at the moment. But something isn't right here. We know we did nothing wrong, but someone threw us onto the chopping block. Either we're being blamed for a huge blunder on the Protectorate's part, or we're being setup for something someone else did.

Sentry stopped in his tracks. Well, he would have—if it wasn't for the agent behind him, who kept pushing him forward. He hadn't thought of that. Someone in the Protectorate could be manipulating events behind the scenes. They could be covering their own tracks while Sentry and his team took the fall for their deception. This was too much.

Finally, they hit the ground floor and were escorted to the exit. At the front, Sentry could see the desk clerk stand up and watch them. The tall, older woman had always been nice to him in his time here. Part of him wondered if he would ever see her again. But he didn't know what to think. Were the cards being stacked against them? Was someone really manipulating things to cover up illicit crimes?

Two agents threw open the doors and they were pushed outside. There they could see a caravan of black vehicles. "Where are you taking us?" asked Sentry.

"We're taking you to an off-site detention center where you will be held for questioning. If things go poorly, you will be teleported to the official Protectorate Headquarters in Germania," a special agent replied.

"Why not just teleport us to the off-site facility?" Sentry's heart was beating out of his chest.

"Because of the situation with you and your agency, we're unsure if we can trust you or your team members. So, that means we will travel the old-fashioned way."

"Well, why—"

"Enough questions!" The agent pushed Sentry against a large black truck, along with Brimstone and Insight. The rest of the team were pushed up against the other trucks. A moment later, a different agent sidled up against them. He smiled from ear to ear, almost to the point of it being unsettling.

"Well, well, well, look what we have here," he said. Then he looked over at the agent guarding them. "Have these kids given you any trouble?"

"No, sir."

"Good, good, good," said the new agent. Then there was an awkward pause. "Brand told me to oversee the prisoner transport for these three."

"Very good, Special Agent Allbright."

"Well, let's light this candle."

With a rough shove, they ushered the agents inside the trucks. The vehicle had a large platform they stepped up on when the doors were opened. Then they stepped into a small containment section that had space them to sit. Sentry slid over to one end and

Brimstone sat next to him, followed by Insight and Codex. Lastly, two unknown agents stepped into the back and sat next to them.

After a long, tense moment, the truck started up. Then they departed to face their trial and potential imprisonment. Uncertainty clung in the air as they left the Guild headquarters. Eyes darted toward each other and then back to the floor. None of them were hopeful in what lay before them. Regardless of the outcome, this would forever change their careers and their lives.

FILE #4

AGENT ALLBRIGHT

The rumble of the truck as it hit the road startled Sentry. They rode on for several minutes in utter silence. No one had the courage to speak. The agents guarding them looked on with a stern coldness. That is, except for Agent Allbright. He had that same creepy smile on his face as he stared at them. Sentry only looked up once or twice, and both times Allbright wore that blood-curdling expression. Immediately, Sentry dropped his gaze like he was studying the floor.

While Sentry sat there, lost in his own downward spiral, he noticed Allbright stand up. A long spear of light sprang from Allbright's hand and he stabbed the first agent with it. Before anyone could react, a second light spear shot out from his other hand and sliced into the other agent as easily as the first one had. Both of the special agents stood there, spikes of pure light protruding from their chests.

For a split second, the handcuffed agents were frozen in fear and confusion. How could this special agent slay his allies in cold blood? The two agents fell down to the ground and remained unmoving. Sentry's eyes were wide as he stared at them. He prayed, he willed them to move. To get up. But nothing. Not even a twitch.

Then, Sentry caught Allbright's gaze, noticing a fire in his eyes. He practically snarled at him, his teeth bared and his brow furrowed. "Well, well, well," said Allbright. "It looks like we have ourselves a situation."

Sentry attempted to lunge at Allbright, but Allbright summoned a light barrier in between them. Sentry slammed into it. With his gift suppressed by the handcuffs, he couldn't do much in the way of offense. Allbright gave Sentry that sinister smile once again. The one showing too much teeth.

"You've really gotten someone really high up in the organization upset with you, so I need to make it look like you four attacked me, and I had to take you out. But unfortunately, you monsters killed two innocent agents in the process."

"How dare you!" Sentry screamed as the last ounce of self-control melted away. Once again, he slammed into the light barrier in front of him, but without an actual gift to use, the barrier didn't even flicker.

"Do you want to do this the easy way or the hard way?" chuckled Special Agent Allbright.

"I'd rather die than go down like this," said Sentry.

"Me too," said Brimstone, standing up.

"Make that three," said Insight.

"I'd like to make it out of this whole situation in one piece," added Codex.

Allbright smiled at the four young agents. Each of them was still bound, so they weren't a threat. Even if they had superior numbers, they didn't have access to their gifts. He could do this quickly or slowly if he wanted. In his mind, he ran through a few quick scenarios. *What's the best way to make the whole scene look like I was attacked?* Then it hit him. He dropped the light barrier. It would be good if he had some actual bumps and bruises to sell the story. Plus, he could use the workout.

"Fine," he said. "Let's have some fun."

Immediately, Sentry rushed at him. He swung his manacled hands at Allbright, who easily parried them with his gift and then slashed at Sentry with his own attack. This forced Sentry to jump back, but he stumbled and rolled backwards as the truck turned. Then he slammed into the back wall. For a moment, he sat there dazed. Both Insight and Brimstone attacked Allbright in tandem.

Although his own attack had failed, it gave him an idea. Sentry got up and took a shaky step forward. It took him another moment to find his footing after his tumble. But he righted himself, and he was set. Like before, he lunged forward. This time, when Allbright slashed at him with his light blade, Sentry threw his hands up. The blade slashed through the handcuffs, slicing them in half.

The two pieces fell to the ground with a loud clank. Allbright stood still for a moment, his mouth hanging open and eyes wide. In his momentary pause, Sentry held up both hands and balled them into fists. As he did, both Brimstone's and Insight's handcuffs broke off. The three of them looked at Allbright with a smirk. Allbright took a step back in fear. His hands started to tremble.

"Listen, the driver is on my side. It was his idea to do it this way," he said.

"The driver is in on it too, huh?" Brimstone asked.

"I mean, yeah. We were going to stage the thing together."

"Interesting," said Insight.

"Tell him to stop the car," said Sentry. "We're getting off."

"I can't let you just leave. They will—"

Brimstone held up a fist. "If you don't let us leave, we will have to hurt you."

Without warning, Allbright turned and slammed his fist against the wall. "Do it. Crash the car!"

A moment later, the large truck sped up. Sentry's heart matched the car's speed as it continued barreling down the road. Everyone in the back pitched forward violently as the truck crashed. Then they were spinning as the truck flew into the air. It felt like the terrifying moment would never end as Sentry tried to focus on not losing his lunch while his ears were assaulted by the sound of crunching metal and shattering glass.

The other vehicles in the caravan swerved to avoid a collision. The truck finally slammed into the guardrail, sending sparks into the air like firework. Then the metal snapped, and the car went over the edge and down into the ravine.

The caravan had stopped now. Several of the agents got out of their cars and began looking around. Some rushed to the edge to look for the truck. A few of the higher ups were calling the situation in while others were blocking off the road. The Guild agents just looked on in horror. Captain V took one look at the scene as best as he could from what he sat and, thanks to his gift, knew exactly what happened. He couldn't explain how he knew, but that was how his gift worked. His intuition was almost never wrong. He listened as the agents outside yelled orders and discussed their next steps.

"Which car was it?" asked a female agent—Agent Brand.

"It was Allbright's truck. The one with Sentry," said another agent.

"I need four teams, now!" Brand yelled as she walked over to the spot where the guardrail had given way. Four agents came up behind her. She looked over her shoulder and nodded at them. They all jumped down the hill. Sliding down the dusty, rocky hillside, they couldn't see much at the bottom because of the smoke and dust in the air. Down below, she could see part of the fender and a shattered rearview mirror, but there was no sign of the vehicle itself.

"Do you see anything, sir?" asked an agent.

"Nothing over here," said another.

Brand scowled. "Just some wreckage so far. Keep moving further down. It must be at the bottom."

The five agents stumbled and slid their way down to the bottom of the ravine. More wreckage littered the ground when they touched down. The air was still thick with dust and debris. Visibility was still terrible. The agents quickly formed a tight pattern as they moved onward.

"You don't think anyone survived, do you?" asked another agent.

"Shut up and keep moving," said Brand.

As they moved through the valley, they finally saw the truck ahead. It was turned so they could see the front. The engine was completely smashed in. It looked like it had been crushed by a boulder. The team wheeled around to the side, ready to check the back. When they came to the side, Brand moved in first. This was her operation, after all. Both of the doors were open. She readied herself just in case of an attack. But as she hopped up into the truck, she couldn't see any signs of the four agents.

She slammed her fist into the metal and bit her lip. She spun on her heel and dropped onto the ground. The other agents were looking at her, ready for their orders. "What do we do?" asked an agent.

"Get a search party ready. We're looking for the four missing agents."

FILE #5

YOUR UNSEEN FRIEND

Four agents sprinted through the rocky valley into the nearby forested area and then stopped for a moment to rest. They had no idea how long they had been at it. The adrenaline pumping through them and the confusion of the crash didn't help. They could have been running for hours or mere minutes.

"Nice job back there, buddy!" Brimstone patted Sentry on the back as they both sat down on a large boulder.

"Thanks," he said. "Instinct just kicked in."

"Well, you held us all in place, so we didn't get crushed as we spun," said Codex. "Honestly, it was most impressive."

"Yeah," added Insight.

Sentry looked over his shoulder. "So, what do we do now?"

"I don't know," said Brimstone. "Are we just going to be fugitives now?"

Codex looked afraid. "Shouldn't we report back to the Protectorate?"

"What about whoever is trying to kill us?" asked Insight. "If we go back, who's to say we won't get stabbed in the back again."

"That's a good point. I don't like getting stabbed in the back. I would vote against getting stabbed in the back, please," said Brimstone.

"Then we go on the run?" asked Sentry. "That's not the life we signed up for. It's not fair to any of you to have to live on the run because of something we never did."

"I say we go after whoever did this to us," said Insight. "Whoever it is."

Sentry ran a hand through his hair. "How do we figure out who they are?"

Insight froze and then looked over her shoulder in the direction they had all just come from. She held her hand up. Then she motioned for them to move. "Let's get out of here," she whispered.

"What's wrong?" asked Codex. "Are there animals?"

"No, I think we have agents after us."

"Insight, try that thing you did to us to make us think you went one way when you went the other way," Sentry suggested.

"Good idea," she answered. "This might be harder since there's more than one mind to deal with, but if I can get one of them, it may work."

She pushed forward to target one of the minds behind them. Once she caught one of them, she entered their consciousness. She then triggered the part of their brain that made them hear things and interpret what they heard. She manipulated it to think the person heard them moving to the east.

Insight was already on the move. "All right, let's not stick around to see if it worked or not. Let's just get a move on, and we'll pray it worked."

Behind them, one of the agents called out, "This way. I heard them moving toward the east."

The four fugitive agents moved through the woods to the west and toward a nearby town.

***

A man watched the wreckage from a rocky outcropping. Although his instinct was to intervene, he remained hidden and just observed. He couldn't be sure what happened, but he had been tasked with monitoring the situation, not to help. Still, he said a silent prayer for the rookie and his friends who were down in the crash. Hopefully, they were alright.

For the last few years, this man had been working in the shadows to uncover the corruption in the Protectorate. He was not an official agent. Not anymore. It was only one of the changes to his life when he died.

He sighed. He was a different person now. Instead of working for the Protectorate, this former agent worked to fix it. The man formerly known as Agent Rikers stalked over to the rock's edge and peered down. He thought about moving down to speak with the agents, but there were guards inside. He had seen them get inside at the Guild Headquarters, and he had followed them the whole way, having been easily able to keep up using his gift of turning into air and mist. It made travel almost simple.

He had no way of communicating with Ein or V, but he needed to find out what was happening. So, instead of trying to reach them, he turned into a cloud of fog and moved down the cliff. He masked himself by rolling under the car. He was practically invisible now. Only the faintest hints of his presence could be detected. He listened from under the truck. He tried to figure out what was going on. He heard a woman screaming for an update and for them to move. Then the five of them jumped down the ledge.

They must be going after the wreckage, either to retrieve them or find the bodies, he thought.

One of the agents stepped away from the rest of the team. She was hiding behind the rest of the trucks, and she pressed the item in her hand up to her ear as she checked for the fourth time that no one was around.

"Sir, yes, we have had a situation," she said into the device. "Well, you said to inform you if anything happened."

There was a pause while she listened to the other speaker.

"Yes, the hit didn't go according to plan. The truck crashed."

She paused again.

"Oh, I didn't think of that. Yes, this could actually be helpful for us. Maybe we can use the crash."

Pause.

"I will, sir. Thank you. I will let you know if we have any developments."

Then she dropped the phone and stomped on it with her foot. She then kicked it into the dirt and tried to cover it as best she could. She walked around to the other side of the vehicle and tried to act nonchalant. Rikers, however, was on the move again. He snapped back into his human form and grabbed the destroyed burner phone. Then he immediately popped into a wisp of mist.

Whatever was on that phone, he wanted to check it out. It might be nothing, but there could be some information on it. From what he was piecing together, there had been an attempt on Sentry's life. Poor Rookie was always getting himself into trouble. Now, he and the rest were gone. Maybe forever. Rikers needed to speak with Ein and figure out the next step.

That meant waiting. And wait he did. Rikers remained in his mist form for over an hour while the vehicles stayed there. In that time, he saw the five agents who went down the ravine return. However, there weren't any bodies. He hoped that was a good sign.

The lead agent yelled out to the rest of the team. "We have four agents on the loose. I want a recon team to go after them immediately. Like yesterday. Let's move!"

A team of agents formed and was sent down the ravine to follow after them.

"The rest of you, let's form up and move out. We still need to get the rest of this team to the base for questioning."

Finally, the trucks were loaded up and they went on their way. Rikers followed them. In less than an hour, they were at a large base. It looked like more of a military base than the normal Protectorate headquarters. The caravan passed through a large security gate at the front. A small team of guards at the gate let the caravan inside and the gate closed behind them. There were a few large hangars ahead of them. There were several large buildings on the base, but Rikers wasn't sure what buildings were what. Maybe they were offices, or they could have been barracks for agents.

Once the trucks were parked, the team of agents removed Ein and V from the vehicles. Another team removed Granite and the other agents from their truck. They were brought into a building that wasn't quite a prison, but it was meant to house people in mass. There were cots and other different equipment for housing people in an emergency.

The guards deposited the members of the Guild inside the room and left. A few of the Protectorate agents were positioned at the door as guards, but none of them were inside. This was his chance. He waited for Ein to be seated off to the side. From inside of the vent, he waited until Ein was alone. Despite the lack of guards, there would most definitely be hidden cameras and security systems in place so he would need to approach Ein in his mist form. But how to make Ein aware of his presence?

Rikers looked around the room and noticed a water bottle on the ground at Ein's feet. Using his mist-form body, he wrapped himself around it. The bottle began to sweat and water droplets formed on the edges from condensation. Then Rikers used that moisture writing on the ground. At first, Ein didn't notice, so Rikers passed by him, causing a shiver to run through Ein. He looked around confused for a moment, and then Ein looked down to see Rikers' message.

It's your unseen friend. What's our next step?

Ein placed a hand over his mouth, so the cameras could see, and then he whispered, "If you can get to the other agents, tell them they need to get to Europe and find Kaze."

Has she made contact?

"Yes, and if they can find her, they might be able to prove our innocence."

I will find them.

"Rikers, if you can't find them, then you need to go to Europe yourself. The four of them might be lost to us."

Understood.

Rikers wanted to write more. To tell Ein that he would find them no matter what. But if they were already in the wind, he would go himself. He would find Kaze and her contact. That together, he and Kaze would prove the Guild's innocence and find the ones behind this. But he didn't have the time to write it in his mist form. It had already taken him too long as it was. But that kind of message wouldn't do much else.

With that, he passed back into the vents and out of the building. The Protectorate agents were already looking for Sentry and the others. If he was going to find them, he needed to move quickly. Once off the Protectorate compound, he sailed through the air toward the crash site. Along the way, he popped out of his mist form and took a breather at a nearby gas station. Although he was able to hold that form for hours, he always felt incredibly thirsty afterwards.

I wonder how much moisture I lost? he thought as he walked into the gas station. *It feels like a lot... Of course, writing notes on the ground probably didn't help.*

After buying a few bottles of water, he downed them all immediately. Ready to continue, he reverted back to his mist form and got to the crash site in good time. There he remained in his fog-like body, moving like an unseen shadow. He followed the tracks and looked over the scene. It had all been cleaned up. The truck was gone now, but it was evident there had been a crash.

His mist form quickly started to shift until his arms, his chest, and then his legs were visible. Back in his human form, he knelt down to examine some footprints. Although, he wasn't the most skilled tracker, he easily found the footprints left behind by the Protectorate agents. He snapped his fingers.

Immediately, he shifted back into mist form and chased after the agents.

THE SEARCH PARTY

The five-person Protectorate team was moving through the forest at a rapid pace. They were all specifically chosen for their gifts. Brink was able to teleport quick but short distances while Bloodhound was able to track anything or anyone using smell. Bloodhound led the team toward the town beyond the forest. Brink teleported to the edge of the woods, looked at the town, and then he teleported back.

"Looks like we have a small town ahead. I think they're headed that way. What does your nose tell you?" he asked.

Agent Aura stepped up, ready for some action. Her sleeves were rolled up to reveal coiled dragon tattoos and she was wearing fingerless gloves. Wick held out his hands. In each palm, a tiny ember flickered. These two had been brought along in case there was any resistance. They'd been given the authority to bring the four agents down if necessary. Lethal force was usually only allowed only in extreme scenarios.

Bloodhound shook her head. "Let's attempt to make contact first. If we can't even find them, then it's a moot point."

"Valid," said Wick. "Let's move out then."

After a few more minutes of walking, they came to the edge of the forest that Brink had mentioned. There they could see the small town, if you could call a gas station and a few fast food restaurants just off the edge of the interstate a town. There weren't too many places for the Guild agents to hide.

"Well, this makes our job easy. Not many places for them to be," said Wick.

"If they are even still here," said Aura.

"What if they just passed it?" asked Brink.

"It's possible." Bloodhound sniffed the air. "I think they're close. My best guess is they're stopping at the gas station for some cheap food, and then they're probably going to try and catch a ride out of town."

The team carefully scaled the rocky cliff and headed to town. As Bloodhound was about to begin the trek down the cliff, she turned back. She could smell something on the wind. Something was different in the air, but she couldn't explain it. Never in her life had she smelled anything like this before. However, she shrugged at the thought. With a shake of her head, she pushed the thought from her mind. She was being silly. So, she turned and continued her descent.

As the team moved down, they noticed that the rocks were all sliding down around them. Bloodhound looked up. Rocks the size of their heads began rolling down the cliff. Then there was a crack. Dirt started to slide down the cliff face, bringing all of the agents with it.

Immediately, Rikers took a chance and sped down the road toward the gas station. If that agent was correct, they should be there. In a matter of seconds, Rikers wheeled around to the far side and popped back into his human form. Then he ran around into the gas station. They were nowhere to be found. For a moment, he weighed his options. Should he scour the aisles and back areas for the agents, or should he take his chances with the next place? He had moments to decide.

Everything inside Rikers told him that they weren't here, so he decided to check another spot. Odds were they had already hit the gas station and were on the move by now. A little further down the road, he saw a mechanic shop. There were several cars in the lot. Some were missing parts, like a fender or a wheel. Others looked like they had been recently repaired. A thought hit him. If he was on the run, he might check out an auto shop to see if he could get an easy ride.

In his mist form, he darted into the large auto shop. Just as he suspected, the four agents were in the back, attempting to hotwire a car. As he popped into his human form, he saw Brimstone leaning into the car through the window and inspecting it. Codex was looking under the hood while Insight was facing the other direction. Sentry's mouth hung open as he turned around to see Rikers. The person he worked with on his first real mission. The one who he had been hoping to help since Rikers had been attacked on his graduation day.

"Rikers," he whispered, a lump forming in his throat. He cleared it and asked, "What are you doing here?"

Now fully human, Rikers answered. "I'm here for you four, actually. Ein sent me to find you."

"Is Ein alright?" asked Insight. "What about the rest of the team?"

"Everyone is fine. They're just holding them in a detention center right now. But he gave me a mission for us to complete," Rikers nodded.

"What mission?" asked Brimstone.

"It's Kaze, isn't it?" asked Insight.

"It is. Her special assignment," answered Rikers. "But we don't have time to talk about it now. We need to get moving. Once we are in a secure location, we can discuss the mission."

Sentry looked over his shoulder. "Do you have a way out of here?"

"No, I was hoping you did." Rikers pointed to the car.

Brimstone snapped. "Give me a minute and I can jump it."

"No time," said Codex. "I will."

Codex moved over to the car and made a turning motion with his hand. Instantly, his technopathy overtook the engine. He told the car to turn on and then the engine silently hummed to life. The team got inside while Rikers slid into the driver seat since he knew where they were going. Sentry, Codex, and Brimstone were already sliding into the back seat as Insight got into the passenger seat.

Rikers stepped on the accelerator and the car shot forward. He cut to the left, and they sped out of the building and onto the road. They could see five agents up ahead. Rikers cursed under his breath. "I thought I may have bought us more time..."

"Who is that?" asked Sentry.

"Protectorate Agents after us?" Insight guessed.

"Exactly. We need to outrun them." Rikers slammed onto the accelerator, and the car launched forward.

Bloodhound ran forward, chasing the car in a futile attempt to catch up to them. If nothing else, maybe she could get their scent so she could track them down later. Meanwhile, Wick summoned his fire-based gift and launched several explosive fireballs at them.

Brimstone looked over his shoulder at the sound. "They have another fire-based gifted?!"

"They aren't that uncommon, Brim," said Insight.

"Oh, right..."

"Are they really attacking us?" asked Codex.

"No, it looks like these are warning shots. None of the shots have even come close to hitting us. I think that's intentional," Sentry said, looking out the window.

Insight nodded. "Most definitely." She looked back and noticed one of the agents was just standing there. Blue and purple light was emanating from her fingertips. Likewise, her eyes glowed a similar shade. *What is she doing?*

The car sped ahead, leaving the five enemy agents in the dust. Their silhouettes grew smaller and smaller until, eventually, everyone in the car lost sight of them.

"Think we lost them?" asked Brimstone.

"I don't think so." Insight turned to face him and Sentry. "One of those agents was doing something. I didn't like it. I think we'll see them again."

Meanwhile, the five agents regrouped. Bloodhound was huffing and puffing from her sprint. "I didn't get much of their scent. Too much fire in the air."

"Sorry about that," said Wick.

"No, don't be. You followed protocol. I was just hoping I could do my part." She looked over to Aura. "So, did you get them?"

Aura nodded. "Oh, yeah. I got them. No matter where they go, I'll be able to track them."

"Good," Bloodhound said. "Now, let's get something to eat. I could go for a breakfast burrito."

FILE #7

IN THE WIND

Riker and the rest of the team drove for as long as the car's electric battery held out and only stopped when they needed to pull over and recharge. They found themselves a small motel where they could regroup. Insight had managed to convince the owner to let them stay for the day and pay later. Inside the crusty old room, the team sat around trying to figure out a plan.

Meanwhile, Insight was doing a perimeter sweep. She walked around the motel, scanning with her telepathy to make sure no one in the area was thinking about any of them. If someone was spying on them, it would be time to leave. But when she finished her sweep, she was pretty certain none of the Protectorate agents had tracked them. Not yet at least.

What was that woman with the glowing hands doing, though? She might be tracking us... She tried to shake off the unsettling feeling as she returned to the room and locked the door behind her.

She dropped her keycard into the bowl on the dresser by the door. "Exit plan?" she asked.

"Back stairwell come down right to the car," said Codex.

Sentry smiled. "I'll run interference while you and Codex get to the car."

"I can follow up with some fire if needed," said Brimstone.

"Good." Insight looked over at Rikers. "And what about you?"

Rikers was laying on the bed. "I will probably follow Codex and you out of the building."

"No, you should be helping with diversion tactics."

"I'm not an agent anymore," he said. "My number one goal is to bring down the one responsible for this. Regardless of what happens, I will see that done. Even if it means leaving the four of you behind."

Sentry stood up. "Easy! We get it, everyone is a little tense. Rikers, you do whatever you see necessary. We'll run our team without you."

"That's not what I meant," he said.

"It sure sounded like that," Sentry said. "Are you with us or not?"

"I am," he said. "I am. But the mission comes first."

"Well, this mission can't happen unless we trust each other. We don't need to be fighting the Oculus and you."

"Understood." He shook his head. *Boy this rookie sure had grown up in the last few years.* He wasn't the scared kid he met back in Dr. Drake's lab under the college. He was a strong, capable young man. No, not young man. He was an adult now. He was a man.

"So, what's this mission that Ein sent you on?" asked Insight.

"You know Kaze was on a secret mission, right?" asked Rikers.

"Yeah, when we were sent on that fool's errand with Quiet, she was sent off to some unknown mission in Europe," said Insight.

"Exactly, but no one was told what she was doing except for the captains and me," he said back. "I was sent with her as backup. But I returned when things grew cold."

"What happened?" said Sentry. "And start from the beginning."

Rikers leaned in. "A few months ago, we received contact with someone claiming to be a member of the Oculus who wanted to defect. In that time, we have learned that she is no on the run. The Oculus found her and she has been forced to go into hiding."

"So, we need to find her?" asked Insight.

"Exactly," said Rikers. "It was after I left that we found out that she was on the run. So, we need to make contact with Kaze and see where she is with finding this contact."

"Alright, where are we headed?" asked Sentry.

"VentoMorto, Italy," said Rikers.

Codex paused. "How are we getting there?"

"That's the tricky part," said Rikers. "Because we're on the run, we don't have a very good way of getting there. We can't teleport or take a normal flight. If we show up anywhere the Protectorate has eye, we're as good as caught."

"So, what do you suggest?" asked Sentry.

"I think we need to separate," he said.

"Separate?" asked Codex. "That's a terrifying idea."

"No, he's right. If we're together, we're more suspicious and more noticeable. But on our own, we may stand a better chance."

"All right, I guess we all go in it alone," said Sentry, somewhat shaking. He had no idea how to help himself get there. His gift didn't lend itself very well to travel, at least not long distances like over the ocean. Even worse, he had no connections that would allow him to travel.

"How do we all plan on getting out of the country?" asked Rikers.

"Easy for me," said Insight. "I'll try and mind manipulate someone into taking me to Europe."

"Lucky," said Brimstone."

"What do you mean?" asked Insight. "You can just contact your dad and get him to send you on a private jet to anywhere in the world."

"Oh right," he said. "I guess I could do that."

"But you should move fast before they question him."

"Good point," said Brimstone.

"Codex, what about you?" asked Sentry.

"I'll try and hack into a private flight or maybe a teleportation trip if I can," said Codex. "Then I'll try and sneak on under a fake name and get there."

"Sounds good," said Brimstone.

Everyone's eyes looked over to Sentry. "What about you?" asked Insight.

"I have no idea. I don't think I have any contacts or allies who could get me into Europe unseen. And I can't fly there from here. My telekinesis would give out, and I would probably drown."

"Yeah, don't do that, please," said Brimstone. "So, what can we do?"

"I wasn't planning on using my gift, but I supposed I could transport us that way," said Rikers.

"You could take both of us as a mist over the whole ocean?" asked Sentry.

"I did it before. That's how I got here last time. I sailed from Britain to Iceland to Greenland and then on to Canada. It wasn't as direct, but I could do that easily."

"Wow, all right, let's go," he said.

"Let's all leave separately. Brimstone will go first, then Codex an hour later, followed by Insight, and then Sentry and I will leave," said Rikers.

Brimstone left quietly, taking a back alley. He made his way to a small private airport where he could use his father's connections to find a flight out. Codex was the next to leave. Insight was about to leave, when she looked over her shoulder. Sentry stood there, looking at her. She gave him a soft smile.

She closed the door and walked out. But before she left, she had to speak with him. But she could never do this in front of the others. So, she did the next best thing. She spoke into his mind.

Sentry- Gabriel, I need to talk to you.

In his mind, Sentry looked up to see her standing there. It wasn't the beaten-up version of her from the real world. This was her real self. No scrapes or bruises. He smiled at her.

What's going on? He asked. *Why all this?* He motioned to the mental scape they were in.

I need to tell you something.

What? Sentry almost sounded exasperated. *Just tell me.*

I've been having these nosebleeds. I am worried that something is going on with my power...my gift.

Gabriel moved toward her. His mental self was there with just thought. He hugged her, his mental-self squeezing her with all of his might. He missed this. Their closeness. In the days after they broke up, the distanced from each other. Serena became the cold, business type. Gabriel on the other hand, had lost part of himself. Maybe, in a way, he was the same. He threw himself into his work.

We can fix this. We can get you healed.

I don't know.

There are plenty of medically gifted doctors out there. It is going to be fine.

I just don't know. I am so scared. I...I've never had anything like this happen before.

I wish I could say, 'I understand.' But we are going to get through this.

Gabriel held her for a long moment. In the real world, it was the blink of an eye. But in their minds, it was hours. When Serena opened her eyes, she realized her hand was on the door. She wiped a tear that was starting to form in her eye. This was no time to go lose herself.

"You okay, Rookie?"

Sentry shook his head. He nodded, tears almost forming in his eyes.

Sentry and Riker left the building in a puff of mist, passing through the ventilation system and out through the pipes. Then they were literally in the wind.

FILE #8

VentoMorto

VentoMorto was a beautiful village on the northern coast of Italy. Its proximity to the coast made for some milder temperatures, but it wasn't the beach getaway that some other southern parts of Italy were. The quaint village was once a hotbed for mafia activity, but that work had largely fell off. Now the major occupation was the green, energy efficient power plant built by the Sagas Corporation.

As the first to arrive, Codex made quick work of finding a proper hideout for them. He was able to hack into a bank app on his phone and rent a small house on the edge of town. There they would be able to meet and plan for their next step of the plan. Insight and Brimstone arrived later that night, but Sentry and Rikers didn't arrive until the morning two days later.

Rikers was completely spent, struggling to walk and leaning heavily on Sentry until they found a small café where they could sit down. Both of them wore a ball cap and sunglasses to try and mask their identities as best they could, but they weren't hidden well enough. As they sat there sipping their espressos, Sentry noticed a television in the window. It was showing the morning news, but then it blacked out. It flickered for a moment with a strange message.

Sentry: 2100 Via Vicolo.

Sentry's eyes widened. At first, he thought they were in trouble. Part of him wanted to get up and make a run for it. But then something dawned on him. Codex. No other person could pull off something like that.

"Stay here," he told Rikers. "I'm going to buy a phone."

Sentry ran down the street to a small bodega. "Do you sell phones?" he asked while trying to catch his breath.

The shop owner shook his head. "No, but the shop next to mine does."

In a flash, Sentry ran out and down to the next shop. Rikers was practically asleep when he returned when he returned with the burner phone.

"You all right?" Sentry asked.

Rikers sighed. "How would you feel if you flew across the Atlantic Ocean?"

"Valid." Sentry turned the phone on and popped in the address. From the browser, he was able to map the destination. After downing the rest of their drinks, they were able to head out to the location. Fortunately, it wasn't too far away from them, and they made it there within the hour.

"Bout time," Brimstone said from the roof. He was sitting on a small balcony.

"If one more person complains about me flying over here, I swear they'll feel my wrath," Rikers growled through gritted teeth.

"He needs to rest. He's about to pass out," Sentry explained.

Insight opened the door. "Let's get him inside then."

Sentry tried to make eye contact with Insight, but she barely even seemed to notice him.

After they put Rikers in one of the bedrooms to sleep, the rest of the team met up. Codex already had a small workstation set up in the main living room. He had a monitor hooked up to a projector that was displaying a map of the city. Once Brimstone sat down, they were ready to begin. Codex stood at the front of the room, pointing his clicker in the air.

He faked coughed into his hand. "Our next step is finding Kaze. Our last intel says that she's somewhere in the town, but we don't know where."

"Do we have any leads?" asked Insight.

Codex typed away. "As of yet, no. But I have been running scans across town for almost two full days. My best guess is that she's in hiding. Which makes me worry."

"Why?"

"Well, if she is in hiding, she could be injured or worse. She might be hiding out because someone is after her. It's hard to say, but I think the situation could be dangerous."

Insight shrugged her shoulders. "Why don't we conduct some surveillance. Maybe we can pick up some clues around town."

"That's not a bad idea," said Brimstone, pointing a finger. "Why don't we do some actual recon around the town and see what we find out?"

"What if spend days looking for her, and we never find her?" asked Codex. "I am not sure if that is the best use of our time. Plus, the longer we stay in one place, the more likely we could be spotted by the Protectorate."

"What if we divide and conquer?" asked Sentry. "Some of us work on doing physical recon in the town, and some of us keep scanning on the machines for her. Maybe if we do both, we will increase of chances of finding her."

Everyone was silent for a moment. Eyes shifted to each other and then back to the ground. No one wanted to be the one to make the final call. Even Insight, who was usually the most dynamic of the group felt uneasy about the situation. This was more tenuous than their normal missions. Not only was the Oculus a very real threat, but they were also on the run form the Protectorate.

Everything's so complicated, but we have to do something. Finally, Sentry spoke up. "Well, if no one has a better idea, I say we do that."

No one disagreed.

"Insight is the best chance we have for finding her on the streets. She can scan for her mentally, so why don't you go on a patrol. Then Brimstone and I can take turns as well. Rikers should stay close to home and rest. He isn't going to recover anytime soon. And Codex, you're able to do the tech work of, like, fifteen people, so you stay here and keep searching."

Insight collected her gear to head out and then went into the bathroom to get ready. She put on a baseball cap and pulled her long hair into a pony tail so she could slip it though the back. She was putting on some oversized sunglasses when she noticed the bleeding again. She must have overexerted her gift in getting to Italy because she had been bleeding on and off again ever since she'd gotten here.

She grabbed some tissue paper to clot the bleeding, hoping it wouldn't do this for too long. *What am I going to do?* Ever since she'd taken that enhancement from Limit Breaker, her body was becoming more and more unpredictable after she used her gift. Headaches, shivers, and, of course, the nosebleeds.

A few minutes later, Insight came out of the bathroom, dressed and ready for her patrol. As she walked to the door to grab her phone, Brimstone looked over at her. She was pretty well covered and appeared nondescript. With her face almost completely covered, she wouldn't be very noticeable in a crowd.

Then Brimstone looked over to the door of the room where Rikers was sleeping. An idea hit him. He got up and grabbed Sentry's arm. "Hey, you do the first run through, okay?"

"What, why?" asked Sentry.

"I'm going to stay here and keep an eye on Rikers and Codex. I've got things covered pretty well, and maybe this will give you two a chance to talk things out."

"I don't think she wants to talk, man. It's over, okay?"

"Just give it a chance."

Sentry huffed. "Fine, I'll do the first run through."

Insight was already out the door when Sentry was ready to go. He followed a few feet behind her, trying to keep up the appearance that they weren't actually acquainted. As they walked down the streets, he even went other directions or took other routes at times. But they always ended up around the same area. Often times they would stop at shops or peruse vendors on the street.

Sentry asked her a few questions, but she never responded. Every once in a while, he would pretend to be a shopper that was showing off a nice item for sale. But she never really paid him any attention.

This sent him down a mental spiral. He found himself cycling through questions, when he finally told himself to stop. He shook his head, hands in fists. He looked up, keeping a visual on her.

Fine. He thought. *We are just coworkers. You just needed an anchor. Nothing more.*

Insight could hear every word of his mental descent. But she couldn't do anything for him. Not now. If things were different, maybe. But they were on the mission. Kaze's life was in the balance. And on top of that, the whole time Insight was actually scanning the area and sending out mental thoughts to Kaze, trying to call to her. However, a few hours went by with nothing to show for it.

Finally, they found themselves in the shadow of the large power plant. They were walking down the street across from it when Sentry looked over his shoulder. Insight looked up to see him staring at the large facility.

"You know, Brimstone was planning on working at a place like that before we got him pulled into this whole agency life," he said.

"Oh yeah, I don't think I can see him working at a normal nine-to-five," she answered.

"Well, I guess his real dream was to fight in the Arena, but his backup plan was to work at one of these clean energy power plants."

"Okay, now that I can see."

"Absolutely." Sentry chuckled. "He was always a dreamer."

Insight stopped in her tracks. "I'm getting something."

"From where?"

"Gimme a minute." She pressed her hands up over her ears, trying to block out the general din of the town around her. She pushed out with her mind and tried to hone in on where the noise was originating. Where was Kaze's mind? After a moment that felt like eons, she looked up and pointed down a back alley that led in the direction of the power plant. Both of them began sprinting in that direction—Insight in front and Sentry right on her heels.

They weaved through alleyways and blind turns, crossed through deserted streets, and ran down stairways until finally, Insight stopped, pressing her hands over her ears to focus in on the source again. Sentry could hear her humming to herself, once again trying to locate Kaze.

"There!" she yelled. "I think she's hurt. Bad."

"Let's go!"

They ran down another street. "Door just to your left!"

Sentry slammed into the door with his shoulder, and they found themselves inside what looked like an old house that had been partially refurbished to act as an apartment building.

"Upstairs," Insight said.

Like a flash, they were both bolting up the stairway taking two or three steps at a time. Then they were at the door. Sentry went in first, ready with his TK shield up. But when he got into the room, there were no enemies. Just a badly injured Kaze. Insight came around and lifted up Kaze's head. When she looked down, she could see Kaze was holding her stomach. Red stained the blue shirt she was wearing, and it was spilling out between her fingers.

Insight pressed her own hands down on the wound. "Get me some towels or sheets, now!"

Sentry grabbed some towels in the small kitchenette a few feet away. He tossed them over before looking for more sheets in what he assumed was a bedroom. He grabbed more and rushed back in. As he placed the sheets over the wound, he used his other hand to check for a pulse. It was faint, but it was there.

"She has a pulse, but it's really weak," he said.

"Kaze," Insight begged, trying to check her pupils. "Can you hear me?"

She was so weak that she couldn't verbally respond, but Insight had another way of getting her answers. In her mind, Insight could see Kaze's mental world. Like most of the other times she entered people's minds, their minds took on aspects of their personality. You could tell a lot about a person's views and beliefs by the kind of mental world they built for themselves. Kaze's was like a gym. Insight opened the gym door to see Kaze on the floor.

"Are you all right?" she asked.

Kaze sat up. "I don't know if I'm going to pull through from this one..."

"Yes, you will. We're here. We'll get you the help you need, all right?"

"It doesn't matter. All that matters now is the mission. You need to get him," Kaze said, standing up.

As she got up, Kaze's body was becoming more transparent. Her body started to flicker in and out, beginning with her fingertips and slowly moving up her arm like she was being engulfed by an invisible monster. It represented her body's consciousness becoming fainter and fainter. They needed to act quick.

"Who is it? Who did this to you?"

"When I was tracking the defector, I realized that I wasn't the only one looking for her. Then this morning, I got into a fight with some of them. Now, I'm worried that the contact is lost to the wind," said Kaze.

"What about the people that you fought with, where are they?"

"They can't be far. I only just got away from them," said Kaze. "I wouldn't be surprised if they are still looking for me."

"Don't worry, Kaze. We will find them and get help. You're going to make it through this." In that moment, Insight was glad the Kaze wasn't a mind reader, because in reality, she didn't know if Kaze really would pull through.

With that, Insight exited Kaze's mind. She looked over to see Sentry peering out the window. "I think we have some people looking for our friend here. This group has been circling the block for a few minutes now."

Insight sighed. "That's what Kaze said. She was attacked by a group that was after the contact as well."

"How do you want to proceed? Are we getting her and getting out, or are we taking these enemies on?"

"If we lose them, then we have no clues to act on. But if we lose Kaze, we can still try and go after them. The safe bet is to tail them." Insight's stomach twisted as she said those words. She didn't even want to think about losing her friend.

Sentry gasped. "But we can't just leave her."

"We won't. I'll stay with her, but you should tail them. Let me connect to your mind so I'll be able to find you."

Sentry nodded. Once he was downstairs, he came to the window by the main door. He peeked out the window. When the group started heading down the road, Sentry exited the apartment building.

FILE #9

TITUS

Like a shadow, Sentry moved down the street behind the three suspects. Although he wasn't trying to stay hidden, he was trying to look unremarkable and nondescript. It wasn't as much about being unseen as unnoticed. As they walked down the street, Sentry acted like he was a tourist shopping or checking different attractions in the town. Insight and Kaze had helped him become better at tailing people over the years.

As Sentry walked past a clothing vendor's stand, he watched out of the corner of his eye. The suspects were meeting up with a fourth person. He groaned inwardly at the prospect of having another enemy to potentially tail or, worse, fight. But then he realized who the new suspect was, and a cold chill ran down his spine.

He turned from the stand and walked further down the road, trying to not stare. After crossing the street, he pretended to shop for some jewelry from another vendor. When he looked over his shoulder, he saw it really was *him*.

It had been some time since he'd seen this man. Last time they had crossed paths, he had tried to kill Sentry. Even before he'd became a full-fledged agent, Sentry had enemies after him. This was one of the first. He had pretended to befriend Gabriel and his friends back in college. And when he had gotten Gabriel alone, he attacked the young agent with every intention of killing him.

Standing there, speaking with the other suspects was Titus Guerrero.

Titus is alive?! Sentry's hand started to shake and his face was hot. He felt like he needed to peel his jacket off or he'd suffocate from the heat. Was his face melting? No, it was just the blood rushing to his face. It was hard for him to just stand there and watch Titus. Last he saw of Titus was when a small cave was collapsing down around them. But here he was, standing there like nothing had ever happened.

Sentry moved from the current stand to a closer one. Like before, he pretended to be shopping, but really, he just needed to get within earshot. From where he stood, he could hear them talking about Kaze.

"And what about you?" asked Titus to one of his accomplices.

"I didn't see her either," she said.

"So, let me get this straight, you got a clean shot on her, but then you let her get away. And now none of you can find her?"

None of the suspects answered. They were suddenly very interested in the color of their shoes. Titus shook his head, then looked at his hands. He pulled them up to eye level, bit his lip, and snarled.

For a moment, Sentry was worried. *Is he about to attack his own people right here and now?* Sentry tried to divert his eyes, but he kept looking back up. He was having a hard time keeping his eyes off of the scene before him. *Is there about to be another attack right here?* But then he seemed to compose himself. He dropped his fists and they uncurled at his sides. The tension started to diminish now that Titus no longer looked like he was about to attack someone, but Sentry didn't let his guard down just yet.

"So, we have no confirmed kill, and now I have to go tell that to my higher ups," said Titus.

"Sorry…uh, sir," he added when Titus gave him a sneer.

"Fine, let's go and get this over with. I'll have to take the heat for this one."

The group headed off in the other direction. Once they weren't looking, Sentry put down the tea leaves he was holding and headed in the same direction, following the same protocol as before. He tried to seem innocuous and used the crowds and tourists to his advantage. Fortunately, the crowds had picked up in the last hour or so. Even though it made it somewhat harder to track them, he now had a beautiful camouflage to move through.

After following them for an hour, it was obvious that the suspects were taking a long way around. Most likely they had been trained in counter-surveillance and were trying to preemptively shake off a tail. However, Sentry had a special trick. He went to his tried and true TK radar gift. He had followed them for long enough that he had gotten a good sense of them with his radar. But what made his trick possible in all reality was the fact that Titus was giving off a telekinetic pressure. Because Titus used his gift in order to move, Sentry was able to pick him out of a crowd. Now, even if he lost visual, Sentry would still be able to have an idea of where he was.

Finally, they came to a massive mansion with a boat dock out front and a large patio overlooking the water. There weren't any visible guards, but they probably had some kind of surveillance system or gifted inside keeping watch. Down the street, he watched them all enter the house and disappear. Now he just needed to figure out how to get inside. From his current vantage point, he could see the house had a street that ran past it and led to the water. That gave him an idea.

Nearby, a vendor was selling fish. He went up to the man and asked, "Do you have any fishing gear or a boat?"

The vendor smiled. "Well, yes, of course."

"Can you take me onto your boat?"

"No, signore." He shook his head. "I need to stay here and sell my fish."

"How about if I buy all your fish?"

In no time, the man was closing up his shop and walking Sentry down to the boat. Sentry handed the man all of the cash he had and told him to keep the change. He just needed to get close enough to the villa's dock. Once they were on the ship, Sentry asked the man to bring him along the coast because he wanted to see some of the villas. They came down the side of the dock and Sentry started to move toward the bow.

"Signore," the fisherman said, "what about your fish?"

"Give them to the local orphanage," Sentry said. Then he turned and jumped off of the boat into the water. He swam underneath the dock, popping up under the house's large patio. He climbed out of the water using a ladder that jutted out of the lake and went onto the patio. From there, he got up higher, but he didn't hop onto the patio just yet. He could sense someone was out front. Expectantly, he clung to the rungs and waited. He pushed out with his radar and tried to get an idea of which direction they were facing. Once the guard turned away, he sprung his attack. He pulled them backwards off the patio and onto the ground. Then he knocked them out. Fortunately, it went smoothly and the guard was out almost instantly.

He then grabbed the guard's clothes and climbed up. Before making another move, he waited to see if his attack had drawn any attention. When he was certain he hadn't tripped any alarms or security, he pressed on. Easily enough, he slipped inside. The villa was dimly lit, resorting to only natural lighting. Sentry moved along the perimeter, fearful there would be more of a guard presence near the center. From here, he could hear a conversation going on. Someone was having a conversation with Titus, but he didn't know who.

Pressing on, he made his way to the next floor. A group was arguing at the edge of an awning that overlooked a large central atrium. He found an alcove which turned out to be a study and hid behind a wall. From here, he could still see and hear the conversation. He pulled in close to the wall and peeked around the side to watch. They were cloaked in black robes. Best he could tell, one was wearing a male pharaoh mask made of gold, another wore a silver hawk mask, and another wore a feminine-looking iron mask. Sentry recalled seeing these kinds of masks in his ancient Egyptian classes. The golden mask looked like the god Osiris, while the hawk mask was probably the Egyptian god

Horus. It took him a moment because he couldn't get a clean look, but the feminine looking mask was most likely Isis.

"So, you haven't made contact with Antonia yet?" asked on the masked villains.

The masked figure at the center spoke. "No, my team did make what we believe was a fatal hit on her, but we lost her." Based on the voice, that hawk-masked individual was Titus.

The feminine masked figure asked, "What do you mean we lost her?"

"She was able to move and run quicker than the rest of our team. She dodged our attacks and got away. We spread out and combed the area, but we weren't able to check every single building. My guess is she bled out in some shack or something," said Titus.

"Our organization hasn't gotten to be where it is at the center of the entire world order by making assumptions and guesses. We make clinical decisions and we carry them out. At this rate, Titus, I wonder if you really are cut out to be part of our inner circle," said the man in the golden pharaoh mask. He had an older, breathier voice that almost sounded familiar.

"Sir, I have bled for the Oculus. I have carried out hits and all kinds of missions for you. We will find Antonia and we will kill her before she is able to do any more damage," said Titus.

"Do you have any clues as to where she is?" asked the woman in the Isis mask.

"Yes, we found where she was hiding out, and it looks like she marked another area where she might be going."

"Where?" asked the man in the Osiris mask.

"Back to her home base in Greece. Where her family's power company started. Atropos."

"Head there now. Wait for her and finish the job," said the male voice. Then he turned and disappeared.

The female figure remained. She leaned in close and pointed a finger in his face. "Don't screw this up, Titus. You aren't indispensable. We can replace you as easily as that." She snapped a finger in his face before turning on her heel.

There was a sound like a pop and the two figures vanished from view. Most likely they had teleported away, and now Titus remained alone. He turned and looked over the edge. Unfortunately for Sentry, he looked right at him. Both of their eyes widened. But where Sentry had shock in his eyes, Titus had nothing but fire and hatred.

Titus threw out a blast of telekinetic energy that exploded around Sentry. He went flying out the window into the water below.

AN AQUATIC ADVENTURE

The cold wet world engulfed him. He sunk down deeper into the depths as the bubbles rose up around him. His baseball hat and glasses were gone now. Probably flung off somewhere when he'd been hit by the wave of TK energy. He looked up to see the glare of the sun. It was a burning coin in the sky now, but it wriggled and warped as the water refracted its light. From its position, it was probably about to set soon.

Then the moment of serene calmness was broken when blasts of energy pierced the water. They whizzed past him, breaking him out of his revere. Sentry turned and swam in the opposite direction. He surfaced near a docked speedboat. He swam over, grabbed the ladder, and climbed up. As the plasma blasts were zipping around him, he rushed to start the engine. In a flash, the boat was off. For a moment, he was relieved to be getting away. But almost immediately, he realized that Titus and his team were after him.

Three other speedboats were already revving their engines right behind him. One of Titus's accomplices was standing on the front of one and blasting large beams of orange energy at Sentry. A few times, Sentry tried to fire back with his own pulses of telekinetic energy, but none of his attacks were successful. Because he was steering the boat, he wasn't able to aim very effectively and was starting to lose ground because he was trying to dodge them. Now other boats were closing in on him, and he had to act. If he didn't do something, they would be right on top of him.

Then, he had an idea. He spun around for a second and pushed out with as much energy as he dared, creating a large wave that wreaked havoc on the boats pursuing him. The wave threw the first one back, while the one behind it ended up doing a nose dive into the water. It popped back up, losing all of its momentum. The third one was able to wheel around and dodge the tidal wave altogether.

As the other boats were dealing with the wave, Sentry was able to speed ahead. But he looked over his shoulder to see that one of the boats was still chasing him. It was two of the accomplices from before. One of the people on the back of the boat was the person who had claimed to have dealt the deadly blow that led to Kaze currently having to fight for her life. Sentry hoped he would get a chance for revenge on that one. Like before, he shot a few pulses of energy at them. The telekinesis wasn't targeted at the boats but again at the water. Large waves and breaks forced the boat to shift and turn this way and that. Hopefully, it would be enough to lose them.

Sentry turned around and slammed on the accelerator. He sped around a corner and lost them for a moment. But then another threat was coming at him. He saw the flashing lights first, and then heard the sirens. The Italian police—polizia—were closing in on him with two boats. He cut the steering wheel to the left and changed directions toward open water. He looked over his shoulder. Titus's crew were heading that way too.

"Ugh..." He sighed under his breath. All of that progress getting away from them was immediately lost.

He had to think of something. A million thoughts flashed through his mind, but nothing was too helpful. Despite his instinct, he realized turning out to sea wasn't a good idea. Out in the open water, he would not be able to evade them forever. So, he decided on another plan. He turned the boat back in a large half circle and headed back toward the two police boats.

The people on the first boat were calling out to him using a loudspeaker. His Italian was rudimentary at best, but he was pretty sure they were calling for him to cut his engine. He shook his head. "Sorry, officers. I can't do that."

He sped right toward them. The police boats were screaming louder now. As Sentry's vessel closed in, the two boats were starting to separate and make some space. Meanwhile, the three Oculus boats were closing in. Sentry let up on the accelerator, trying to get all the boats closer to one another before he made his move. In a matter of seconds, the Oculus boats had caught up just as he was speeding closer to the police ships.

It was time.

Sentry pulled at the water with all of his telekinetic power. He created a wave that sent the speed boat flying into the air. Sentry's boat, which was also in the air now, sailed over the police ships. The police and the Oculus boats were on a collision course. The police jumped ship as two of the Oculus boats crashed into it. Titus used his telekinesis to throw himself up into the air as his ship crashed. He flew up in a shaky arc into the third boat.

With a splash, Sentry landed back in the water. He turned to look back at the wreckage. Two of the Oculus ships were in a blazing inferno, but the furthest one was now wheeling around. Instinctively, Sentry groaned when he saw Titus still in the picture. The last boat began to close the gap.

Sentry turned the wheel and aimed his boat toward the dock ahead. There were more pleasure ships, yachts, and luxury cruisers stationed there, so Sentry decided to try and lose them in the crowd. He wheeled around a massive cruise ship and then quickly wrapped back around two yachts. Then he whirled through a series of pleasure boats that were anchored just off the shore. Several wealthy sailors yelled or gave Sentry dirty looks as he wheeled around them.

But the distance wasn't enough. Titus could still wreak havoc from a long way off. Despite the range between them, Titus was yelling orders for his pilot to push the boat harder. The ship didn't fall for Sentry's tricks and they simply wheeled around and was able to spot him. His zig-zagging and flying around here and there didn't help him when his enemy could attack from a distance. Titus held out his hand and a surge of telekinetic force pulsed outward. Several of the boats toppled over and waves started to rip through the waters. Sentry felt the pressure behind him.

He looked over his shoulder and saw the waves lapping up over his boat. He held on for dear life as a massive tidal wave slammed into him. He was drenched, but somehow, he remained afloat. But then the boats behind him started crashing into each other. Then a speedboat went flying and almost crashed into him, just barely missing him.

Immediately, his eyes went wide in shock. His heart raced and he tried to punch the accelerator. That first wave was just the beginning. A wave behind him toppled over three large cruise ships and all of the large pleasure ships. A yacht almost crushed him. If he hadn't shielded himself, the metal ship would have killed him instantly. The wave picked him and the ship up and threw him into the dock. The boat smashed through the wooden pier and through several other ships. The ship then collided into a large warehouse at the end of the dock. Sentry's boat smashed through the first support beam like it was nothing and the second was bent.

Sentry huddled under the steering wheel, encased in a shield of TK energy. But all was not safe yet. Immediately after colliding with the second beam, he looked up to see the beam snap and fall on him. Instinctively, he covered his head. The beam hit the shield, bending further, and then he heard a loud cracking sound. Another beam broke under the strain of the weight. He looked around as the last support beam cracked and broke under the pressure. In no time, the entire building was coming down on him.

Outside, Titus and his ship were sailing past. He watched the wave slam two more ships into the top of the warehouse where Sentry was hiding. He smiled as he watched the entire structure crash down around him. He turned the boat around, and they sailed off.

"Should we head back to the villa, sir?" asked his accomplice.

"No, the villa is burned now. It will probably be swarming with polizia or worse, neighbors."

"Then on to the base?"

Titus nodded. "Probably our best bet now. There we can rendezvous with our team and schedule a teleportation to Greece. We need to catch up with Antonia before she makes contact with any other agents."

The boat turned and headed down the coast toward their base. From there they would be able to get out of town before anything got more chaotic. Unless anything else happened, they were never coming back to this town ever again. Titus then looked over at his accomplice.

"Tell Rocco to blow the villa. We're done with this town. I don't want any evidence we were ever here."

"Understood." He grabbed his phone and dialed a number. "Rocco, use the gas. Blow up the villa. Then meet us at the base."

Then he tossed his burner phone into the sea.

FILE #11

FROM THE CRASH

Everything was dark. A few spotlights moved here and there, but they seemed to be swallowed up in the deep darkness of the wreckage. Smoke billowed into the air and debris littered the ground in a watery mess of destruction. Ships and pieces of the pier were scattered around the warehouse. Inside, a stirring silhouette appeared in the form of mist. It moved through the shattered glass and fit between the bent metal. The mist scanned through all of the debris for the lone body in the destruction. Finally, Rikers found the unconscious body. In a movement that only a gaseous form could perform, it swooped down and wrapped around him. Then the body disappeared in a cloud of fog.

Blackness was the first thing, Sentry saw when he came to. The lights were just faintly on in the next room, giving just the barest view of his surroundings. He turned his head to see a form moving toward him. At first, he tried to react, but his body was sluggish. He was sore all over.

"It's just me, Sentry," said Brimstone.

"Wh—where am I?" he asked.

"You're back at our hideout. Rikers found you in a collapsed building."

Sentry sat up with more effort than it should have taken. "Yeah, that's right. I ran into Titus. Remember him?"

"He's still alive? How?"

Sentry shrugged. "I mean, how am I alive after a warehouse fell on me?"

"Good point."

Sentry swung his arms off of the bed and made an effort to stand up. But he realized he would need a minute before that happened. "I need a minute, but I know our next destination."

"Where?"

"Greece. A city called Atropos."

"All right, I'll get the team ready and we will head out as soon as we can."

"Yeah, you go do that. I need a minute…" Sentry paused. "Wait, what happened to Insight and Kaze?"

Brimstone froze and his hands dropped to his side, but he didn't turn around. "When I got there, it was too late. She was already gone."

Sentry's fists started to shake in frustration. Another friend lost. One more name to add to the list of people hurt because of this Oculus group. Now If Sentry needed motivation before, now he had it. It was up to him to bring this disgusting group down. With shaky legs, he got to his feet. His face was a slowly cracking mask. Behind the facade of strength and anger was a soul screaming out in pain and anguish.

"Let's go."

***

Marcus walked from his office toward Bartholomew Zeno's room. He needed to speak with him. Each step was done so with purpose. The man that strode down the halls was one born for power and wealth. He had taken the power he was given and used it to grow an empire. An empire that benefited him in more than one way. His company, Pharis International, was the dominant hiring agency in the world. All over the world they paired gifted individuals with the perfect company for them. However, he used the company for another more nefarious goal. But the world didn't know about this goal. Only those in the Oculus knew about that.

Finally, he pushed the door open. Zeno looked up from where he sat at his desk, somewhat confused. "What is wrong, Marcus?"

"Pius failed," he said. "Again."

Zeno hung his head. "What are our contingencies?"

"The Protectorate chairman's seat is about to open. We can always push for a bid for you to be elected."

"I would prefer to have less of attention drawn to myself. All of the checks in place for the chairman's seat would make it hard for me to do all of this," Zeno said.

Pharis hummed. "Then we can continue to pursue a means of getting the chairman's position in our pocket, which is always a difficult and dangerous process."

Zeno nodded. "Should we try another avenue?"

"It's too early to tell," said Pharis. "But that brings me to my next point. What do we do about Pius? He's been hurting the Oculus for the last few years now and has nothing to show for it. I think we should enact an immediate removal."

Zeno crossed his arms. "You know what that means, don't you?"

Marcus nodded. "I do. I will enact it myself."

"Very well. Call in the rest of the committee members."

Marcus returned to his office to make the preparations. He personally contacted all of the members of the council and almost called Aria's son, Titus, but then remembered he was on an assignment. Plus, he wasn't in high standings just yet. He was more of a seat filler, at least in Marcus's mind.

"Goodness, so few of us now," he said after calling Pius.

With Drake gone now, Romulus incarcerated, and now Antonia on the run, the Oculus was in a dangerous situation. Their station as a major player in the world was in jeopardy. *Maybe it's a bad idea to remove Pius from the organization,* he thought. *But weakness cannot be allowed. If we continue to allow failure in the Oculus, then what will our power mean?*

"No, Pius needs to go."

He got up and went over to his armoire—a large wooden piece of furniture with a dark walnut finish. He opened the doors and looked at his bronze-colored falcon mask. It represented the Egyptian god, Ra, the sun god. As he placed the black robes over himself, he thought about that. *Maybe, like Ra was the god of the sun, I could be the bringer of a new dawn for Oculus.* Zeno might no longer be fit to lead. Pius was an incompetent fool. They would need some new blood in the Oculus, and Marcus would be the one to bring it.

He placed the bronze mask over his face and exited the room. He walked down a dark hallway to the meeting room. As usual, they met in the dark room with the long mahogany table. Zeno, wearing his golden Osiris mask, sat at the head of the table. Beside him was his most trusted now that Romulus was gone. Jules "Lightbringer" Majors sat down in her mask. Across from her was Marcus in his Ra mask. He looked over at Zeno and as usual, he longed to be in that seat. One day, he would, but he didn't know how that would happen. Not when Zeno literally didn't age. Sure he was over one hundred years old, but he was still in the body of a sixty-year-old. Still, Marcus knew that, one day, the Oculus would be his.

Finally, the man of the hour arrived. Pius came into the chamber, and all of the Oculus members stood up. Pius walked to his seat, but before he could sit down, everyone backed away from their seats and walked over to the large circle painted on the ground. They all stood on the circle.

Finally, Bartholomew said, "Alexander Pius, you have been summoned her to face a trial."

"Trial? What do you mean?" he asked in his silky smooth voice.

"You have been part of our organization for some time, but you have not pulled your weight in that time. Now, there are those who question not only your ability, but your motivation to see this organization prosper."

Pius pushed his chair back with such force that it toppled backwards with a loud bang. "I want to see my accuser, then!"

Marcus stepped up. "It's me. I am the one who thinks you're unfit to wear that mask and sit on this council. You are a waste of space."

Pius wheeled around the table and approached Marcus. Looking at him, Pius attempted to play his one and only card. His gift was the ability to manipulate a person's emotions and control them. "Marcus, my friend, how long have we known each other?"

Marcus didn't allow him to say another word. He threw a punch and Pius's copper mask fell to pieces on the ground. Then Marcus ripped the off his robes. Pius stumbled back, falling to the ground.

"You just signed your own death warrant. Now you die." Before his opponent had the chance to get up, Marcus punched Pius in the face over and over. Then he kicked him in the ribs.

The remaining members of the Oculus stood motionless in the circle. Aria looked away for a moment. But Zeno grabbed her shoulder and said, "No, Aria. We have to watch."

She slowly turned back to face the fighting, but she closed her eyes inside her mask. She couldn't stomach the violence. It was too much for her. But the sound was worse. Much, much worse.

FILE #12

ATROPOS

The team arrived in Greece under the cover of night. Rikers was able to transport them quickly in his mist form, and it felt like nothing compared to his previous trip. They touched down in the city of Atropos, another coastal city with a beautiful bay. The city was named after one of the three Fates, who gave and took life by cutting a single cord. Sentry found it interesting to name a city after one of the Fates, but it probably harkened back to a different time. Similar to how Athens was named after Athena, the people from this city must have been ardent believers in the hand of fate. Sentry found himself hoping they would be the masters of their own fates on this mission.

As before, they were able to purchase a small place to hide out, thanks to Codex and his gift. This time they rented a large extended-stay hotel room on the top floor. From there, they were able to see the part of the city that bordered the power plant. They were hoping that was where Antonia was hiding out. Once Codex was set up, they started planning their next step.

"So, I guess we just follow the same plan as last time," said Sentry.

"It worked last time. So, we might as well," added Insight.

"I need to rest," said Rikers. "Feel free to get started without me. I just need a quick nap."

"Sure thing, Rikers," said Sentry. "You get some rest. We'll get started."

When Rikers went to find the bedroom, Insight turned to Codex and whispered, "Last time he said that, he was out for hours."

"Well, can you blame him?" Codex shrugged. "He flew halfway across the world in the better part of a week."

"I guess that's true. Well, what do we start off with?"

Sentry drummed his fingers on the armrest of the couch. "Why don't we take some shifts while getting Codex's gear set up, and the rest of us can get some rest. Then we hit it really hard at first light."

"You don't want to start now?" Brimstone was practically vibrating with energy, his right leg bouncing up and down as they talked about their next move. Sitting still wasn't something he excelled at, to say the least.

"Sentry's right," said Insight. "It's the middle of the night, so she's probably asleep. We'd have better luck in the in the morning."

"Sounds good," said Brimstone. "I'm still wired from our flight. I'll take the first shift."

"That's probably a good idea," said Codex. "You unload the bags. I'll take the next shift and put it together."

Without another word, the team either got to work or went to find a bed. Everyone except for Insight. Her nose was bleeding again, but she didn't understand why. She wasn't even exerting that much power, so why was it acting up? Instead of heading to bed, she decided to sneak out. Fortunately, everyone was preoccupied. Or so she thought.

Brimstone spotted her on her way to the door. "Where are you going? It's super late."

Then she did something she told herself she would never do. She pushed out with her mind and influenced Brimstone with her telepathy. "I'm just going to run and get some coffee for tomorrow. There's a coffee maker in the kitchen, but we don't have any coffee."

He'd spent a lot of his time in hotels because of his father's career, so he obviously knew most hotels supplied each room with coffee. But it didn't matter that he knew that. In that moment, he completely believed her.

He shrugged. "All right, be careful."

After heading down to the ground floor and exiting the hotel, she went to a small walk-in doctor's clinic down the street. She buzzed the door and was let inside. After waiting in the office for a few minutes, she was brought in to speak with the on-call doctor. The doctor came into the room with a tablet and sat on a rolling chair next to Insight, who was sitting on an exam table.

"What seems to be troubling you?" she asked.

"I'm having some strange symptoms. I worry they might be connected to my gift."

The doctor hummed quizzically. "Can you list them for me?"

"Yes, let's see. It's usually fatigue, some dizziness, and headaches. But once in a while, I also get these really bad nosebleeds."

"Interesting. And what makes you think it is tied to your gift?"

"It's usually tied to when I use my gift," she said. "But it seems to be getting worse."

"Well, it if is tied to your gift, my recommendation would be to stop using your gift starting now. You need to go into a hospital and get a full workup immediately. I can schedule an appointment now."

"I'll be leaving soon, but I'll check in with the doctors back home."

"Ah, yes, I can tell you are from America with that accent."

Insight nodded. "I am."

The doctor crossed his arms. "Well, please get this looked at immediately. Something like this could be serious, so you should err on the cautious side."

"I will."

The doctor stood and prepared to leave. "There is a treatment that might help. It involves a stasis field. It might help. Look into it when you return home."

The doctor left, and Insight grabbed her things. She walked out into the night once again with what felt like the weight of the world on her shoulders. As she walked, she thought back to the day this issue started. Limit Breaker had come to her with the proposition to increase her power so she could defeat Quiet. On their own, the agents wouldn't have been able to defeat him because he had a piece of venisium. So, of course she did it. It was that, or risk losing her friends.

But now, she was facing these health problems—apparently the price for saving her friends. It wasn't fair.

Although they had the mission at hand, she couldn't focus so she spent a few hours aimlessly walking the foreign streets. This was her chance to sleep, but how could she sleep with this weighing on her head? As such, she found herself exploring the older side of Atropos, walking up to the acropolis and down the stone walkway by the temples. There she saw the temple to the Fates.

Maybe I'll be able to change my fate, she thought as she looked at the temple and a feeling of hope stirred in her chest. *I'm in control. Not this sickness.* She refused to allow this ailment to be the thing that dictated her life.

After a few hours of contemplation, Insight finally headed back to the hotel room after remembering to stop by a coffee shop and grab coffee. She snuck back into the room and was in the kitchen when Codex ran into her.

"Oh, did you have a good rest?" he asked.

"Um, yeah, it wasn't bad."

"Well, I think we're just about ready to begin," said Codex.

Insight looked out the window and saw the sun starting to rise over the horizon. She sighed heavily as she realized she wouldn't be getting any sleep today. But that was her cross to bear. She'd made her choice.

The team met in the main room and looked at Codex's setup. He already had a large map of the city pulled up.

"I have taken a few cues from our last mission. So, I've tried to make some adjustments. I've already scanned the entire city's security system for this Antonia Sagas." Codex pulled up a few pictures of her. She was tall woman with a rounded figure and curly, black hair.

"So that's our Oculus member?" asked Brimstone. "She's pretty cute."

Sentry nudged him hard with his elbow. "Focus, Brimstone."

He rubbed his side. "Sorry!"

Codex cleared his throat. "As I was saying, she's the new head of the Sagas energy company. They are one of the biggest energy suppliers in the world."

"So, the situation is more of a search and rescue than a find and capture, right?" asked Brimstone.

"Yes. She could help us bring down the entire organization, so we need her alive."

"What were you saying about scanning the city's security systems?" Insight asked, blinking sleep from her eyes.

"Right, I've scanned a few security systems across the city from the last few days, and I found a couple of partial checks that could have been her in this part of town." Codex pointed to the northwest portion of the map. "I think we'll have the best luck starting here."

"This is great work, Codex." Insight smiled. "We should be able to minimize our time out there and get out of here."

Codex turned back to the map, "Let's start here and we will move out from there."

Insight, Brimstone, and Sentry headed for the district near the power plant. Hopefully they would be able to find Antonia and get out of town quickly. At least, Sentry hoped they would. Maybe this whole situation could be behind them when they got her testimony. Living on the run was exciting, but it wasn't the life

Sentry had planned for himself. It wasn't why he'd stuck out four years of college and a year at the Protectorate Academy.

They went down one street, and then they moved toward the next. After searching a few streets, Insight held up a hand for a few moments before waving the others over. She looked up at a building. "She's up there."

The building was down the street from the alleyway where they were standing. The structure stood out among the other more gray steel buildings. It was a luxury apartment complex with large white stone sides. Beautiful sconces lit each balcony in a dim glow, reflecting of their black iron railings.

"Not exactly unassuming," said Brimstone.

"No, probably not the best hideout. But hopefully she's still safe," said Sentry.

A voice rang out from behind them. "Thank you for showing us the way!" The three of them looked back to see Titus holding up his hand. "We didn't know where to look, so we looked for you. I figured you would be able to track her."

Then he slammed his hand down and a force of telekinesis ripped away at the building behind them. The whole front of the building was torn off and the entire side collapsed, burying everything in its path. As three stories of rock, glass, and brick crashed down around the agents, Titus turned and headed toward the apartment complex.

ON THE RUN

Immediately, Sentry stepped between his friends and shielded them. "Anyone got a way out of this?" he asked through gritted teeth.

"On it!" Brimstone was already pressing his hands down on the asphalt beneath them. It started to melt in a puddle like sludgy tar. Finally, the entire ground around them melted away, creating a large hole to the sewers. "Move, move, move!"

Insight dropped down into the soupy grime of the sewer first. Brimstone looked at Sentry. "Ready?"

"You first. Then I'll drop down behind you."

"All right." Brimstone paused. He turned back, "If you even think about pulling some heroic nonsense like staying behind, I will end you."

Brimstone dropped down into the darkness. Now that everyone was clear, Sentry moved to the hole while still holding up the massive pile above him. It was almost too intense for words. He felt like he was about to collapse. And he was. He dropped down into the hole and then dropped the shield.

As soon as he hit the ground, he yelled, "Run!" Smoke and small pieces of rubble dropped into the sewer around them. "Don't stop!"

They all kept running until they came to the next exit and saw a ladder leading up to a manhole cover. Brimstone jumped up and was at the top in a flash. Sentry pushed out with his telekinesis and leapt up the ladder while Insight quickly climbed up behind him. They exited the sewer in a matter of moment and were on the hunt for Titus.

Titus was out of sight, but they knew where he was heading. Brimstone was in the lead with Sentry hot on his heels. They were about halfway down the road when they saw Titus and two of his goons pulled Antonia into a black truck. A fourth person was revving the engine. The others jumped into the back and the truck sped forward.

Sentry tried to attack, but he was spent. Luckily, Brimstone wasn't. He threw out a fireball that exploded in front of the vehicle. Brimstone smiled as he ran up on the car. However, his glee was short lived. The truck was only momentarily delayed. They revved the engine and blew through the fire without taking major damage.

Realizing they needed to catch up to them, Sentry pushed out to a nearby car. He grabbed control of the ignition, turned the vehicle on, and then forced the doors open as they ran up to it. In no time, they were in the car and on the move. The car sped toward the large black truck and the two vehicles raced down the street. The truck turned left and then right a few times, trying to dodge the agents.

In a few moments, the vehicles were out of the town and driving through the rocky countryside. There were different archaeological digs on the outskirts of town and the remains of old stone and marble temples and courts littered the area. The black truck turned and drove down one of the excavation sites. They roared past freshly dug holes and wheeled around a large bulldozer.

Titus pulled on the bulldozer with his mind and threw it toward the agents' car. Sentry pushed back and threw it into one of the large holes. It crashed into a recently excavated statue. Sentry's eyes widened. *Whoops,* he thought. *Someone's going to be very upset when they get here.*

The large truck swerved when it came to the ledge of a small cliff, but Sentry revved the engine and crashed into them. Both cars went over the edge and rolled over the short cliff onto another excavation site. Despite being banged up and smoking, both cars were still drivable. The large truck took off first. Sentry followed close behind them, hitting them again with the car.

"You know, we're supposed to be *protecting* that girl!" Insight pushed her hair out of her eyes.

"Sorry, I thought that would stop their vehicle." Sentry said as he made another sharp turn.

"Let's take out the wheels." Brimstone popped his head out the window and lobbed another fireball at the wheels. The first wheel he hit didn't explode. His eyes widened and his mouth hung open for a second. He snapped his fingers and threw another fireball at it, but the explosion barely left a mark on the car. Brimstone pulled himself back into the car. "I think that car's got some kind of special plating. Even the wheels seem to be fire resistant."

Insight raised an eyebrow. "Are you going to let that stop you?"

"Good point."

Brimstone climbed out once again. Instead of a fireball, he held out a hand and released a flamethrower at one of the wheels. Gouts of flames roared around the wheel. It took some time, but it eventually melted under the extreme temperatures. The pressure caused an explosion in the wheel well as the wheel tore apart, sending pieces everywhere. The truck fishtailed. Sentry then pulled on it with his mind, slowing it to a stop.

Immediately, Insight and Brimstone got out of the vehicle. Likewise, Titus jumped out of the truck and used his own telekinesis to throw the car door at Insight. She just barely dodged it as she rolled on the ground. Sentry slid out of his seat and launched the same car door back at him, knocking one of the accomplices down. Titus didn't appreciate that. He returned fire by tearing the hood and back door off of the car and hurling them at Brimstone. The first missed, but the second slammed into its target. He went flying back into the car and then fell to the ground.

Two more accomplices came out of the truck and rushed toward Insight. Sentry was locked in a telekinetic struggle with Titus, so Insight moved to intercept. She pushed out with her mind and targeted the accomplices. Both of them looked around, confused. Pain shot through her head. The same headache that had plagued her since Limit Breaker had unlocked her power. She winced. Although the pain was intense, she didn't break concentration. The two goons were now aimlessly walking around, still confused and bewildered. One of them fell off the side of the rock face into a large ravine. The other one fell down into the pit shortly after, tumbling down the steep hill.

Then she dropped to her knees and lost concentration. *Hopefully, they're down because I'm done...* She dropped down to all fours and saw drops of blood on the ground. Touching her nose, she felt a dribble of blood. The world spun when she tried to get up. It didn't quite make sense to her foggy mind. But then she was falling into the dirt. In a matter of moments, everything went dark.

"Looks like it's just you and me," said Titus. "It's been awhile, hasn't it?"

"Yeah, looks like you haven't turned over a new leaf, huh?" asked Sentry.

"Not even a little bit. I am just about a full-fledged member of my organization. Maybe you've heard of it. We call ourselves the Oculus."

"I have, as a matter of fact. We're actually trying to bring her in so we can take down your whole criminal organization." Sentry motioned over to Antonia.

Titus pushed back with his telekinesis. The two were a few feet apart, but their mental energy was colliding in a torrent of telekinesis. The faint blue hue of Sentry's telekinesis clashed against the almost purple tinge of Titus's, crackling and hissing. Titus scoffed. "How about we up the stakes, then?"

Pushing out with his mind, all of his energy was directed at the car. The car inched further and further toward the edge. If he couldn't get away with Antonia, he would have to take her out. Having her out of the picture would be better than her getting away. He pushed out further, but his focus was divided. Sentry was forcing him to divert his attention, so he wasn't able to crush the car as easily.

"NO!" Sentry pushed back at Titus. The force knocked Titus off balance. Then Sentry was able to move in between Titus and Antonia. She was still handcuffed inside of the car that was

He had a reckless idea, but it was all he had. He diverted the energy sparking around him to the ground and the cliff side started cracking. He and the car started to slide down the sheer hillside and away from Titus.

As the rock ledge fell, Sentry waved. He hoped to goad Titus into following him and leaving his friends alone. And it worked. Titus jumped down the broken hillside and slid after Sentry. Sentry didn't waste any time. He opened the car door, grabbed the handcuffs, and slid them off of Antonia. When they got to the bottom, they began to run.

"Here, this way!" Sentry yelled.

"No, follow me!" Antonia said, running in the opposite direction. "I know this town like the back of my hand."

Sentry thought for a moment, but decided to trust her. He nodded at her, and the two began to run away. Antonia helped him sneak through the alleys and down back streets. Finally, they made their way through the tunnels and down through the train station. They did some train hopping and eventually got out of the town.

As they rode away, Sentry looked back and sent out a single thought. He hoped Insight would hear him.

FILE #14

PUZZLES

Antonia led him to the caboose where they could speak privately. Sentry closed the door behind them and looked out the door window. Then he checked the other windows. He couldn't see anything in the train tunnel, but it was a force of habit. After he'd checked them, he joined her. The two of them sat on a bench seat that faced the entrance. Sentry fidgeted for a few minutes as he sat there, trying desperately to look calm.

"Is this your first mission?" she asked, somewhat annoyed.

"No, actually. I've actually been an agent for a few years."

"Really?" The surprise in her tone was something Sentry appreciated.

"Yes, really."

"Do your missions really go this poorly every time?" Antonia crossed her arms.

"Uh, well, more than you would expect."

She stood up, brushing her hand through her hair. "My word, what have I done? I come to the Protectorate for help, and I find myself with a bunch of foolish children!"

"That's not exactly fair. You don't know the whole situation," Sentry said, standing up to face her.

"Well then enlighten me, agent."

"There was a situation…" He paused. "We were attacked by someone inside the Protectorate. Instead of having our full team and all of the resources of the Guild, we are running this operation with our hands tied behind our back and with no support."

"What do you mean 'someone inside the Protectorate'?" she asked.

"My guess is that someone high up in the Protectorate wanted to stop us from doing whatever we were doing." Sentry was becoming more dejected as the realization of everything hit him. His own organization was trying to take him out. The people he'd worked to help were now trying to stop him.

Antonia studied his face. In a matter of moments, her own demeanor shifted. She realized then that he was upset by the situation. She started to speak, but stopped herself.

Sentry clenched his fists. He looked up from the ground and stared directly into her eyes. "I know it seems like we are fouling this up, but it's not just our job. This is my life. They aren't just trying to take you out. Whoever this is, they are after me too. I'm going to stop them or I'll die trying."

"Well, that's more like it," she said. "Now, let's make sure we are heading in the right direction."

Sentry followed as Antonia walked to the back of the train car. "Where are we going?" he asked as he sat down across from her.

Reflexively, Antonia looked over her shoulder. She realized they were in the car alone, but still her reaction was to be wary. "We're heading to a safe house. My parents set it up for me before I was even born. But I'll tell you more when we get there. Until then, let's rest up."

Sentry laughed. "Good luck with that." He didn't think there was any way in the world he would sleep. But he was wrong. Whether it was the exhaustion from the day or the rhythmic cadence of the train, he fell asleep shortly after. It wasn't until the train came to a stop that he realized his error. He shot up with a start and looked around, certain they were under attack, or worse that Antonia had been captured. But there were no enemies. Just an empty train car. He turned to see Antonia looking up at him, amused.

"Ready to go, agent?" she asked, trailing off. "What is your name?"

"They call me Agent Sentry," he said.

"Ah, are you some kind of guard or something?"

"I mean, not technically, but my gift does enable me to protect people pretty well."

Antonia nodded. "Well, we're at the end of the line. We need to take a boat next."

They left the train and then walked out of the station and into a beautiful coastal city. They were near a port, where Antonia had arranged for them to get onto a boat. It was a small fishing boat with no one else on it. But what was strange was that the man seemed to know Antonia, and he immediately let her on the boat. But Sentry seemed to be on the fisherman's bad side. *Is this man here just to wait for Antonia and sail her to wherever she needed?*

When they were finally out at the sea, Sentry asked her about it. "So, what is this fisherman's deal? Is he your chauffeur?"

"Kind of," she said. "He's on retainer, and he receives a salary to stay at this port every day in case of emergency."

"Wow, really?" Sentry blinked in surprise. "That seems like an easy job."

"Unless he's ever found out. Then it won't be."

Sentry nodded. "Ah, good point. Easy doesn't necessarily mean safe."

Sentry moved to the front to keep an eye out until the fisherman called them down below deck. Antonia went down first, while Sentry took one last look around. Once he was satisfied that no one was around, he walked below deck, which appeared to be the fisherman's living quarters. There was a small bunk against the wall as well as a kitchenette and a small door leading to the restroom.

"All right, come here, laddie," the fisherman said in a gravely accent.

"What's going on?" he asked.

"Pola is going to teleport us to my island," Antonia said.

The old man sneered at Sentry like he didn't appreciate the fact that he had to teleport Sentry as well.

"Then why the whole boat thing?" asked Sentry.

"To cover our tracks. Of course."

Sentry paused and thought for a moment.

But Antonia didn't wait for him. "All right, Pola. Are you ready?"

"Always, ma'am." He held out his hands and touched Sentry and Antonia. "Be safe," he said. Then they were gone.

Pola hobbled back up onto the deck. He shuffled over to the wheel and took the ship back into port. When he arrived, he pulled in at his normal spot. After getting his boat docked and tied up, he made his way off of the boat. The old harbormaster looked over at Pola and waved. "Pola, there seem to be a few friends of yours waiting for you."

"Friends? What friends?" he asked.

"Over there," the harbormaster said, clenching a pipe in his teeth.

Pola looked over to see a young Hispanic man that he didn't know walking up to him. "Hi, Pola. It's been awhile. Remember me? It's Titus."

Pola's eyes widened.

***

Sentry and Antonia appeared on a stone pedestal in a beautiful wild garden. Sentry spun around to look at the vibrant flowers. Past the flowers was a vast ocean. He couldn't see land anywhere, but they were on a remote island in the middle of nowhere.

"Where are we?" he asked.

"It's an island in the middle of the Mediterranean called Scylla."

"I've never heard of that island before."

"No one has. It's too small to be on any maps, and there's nothing here other than a small patch of dirt and rock."

"What about this garden?" Sentry continued to look around.

"It's nothing. Just some plants to keep this hidden." Antonia pointed to a small hatch hidden in the stone. Sentry turned to look at it and then knelt down and tapped on the metal door. It echoed with a loud *thunk*.

He looked up. "How long has this been here?"

Antonia knelt down and started turning the circular wheel on top of the hatch. Sentry helped her turn it as she said, "My parents built this around the time I was born I think. They never brought me here, but before they died, they told me about it."

"Is it a bunker or a safe house?"

"Both, really."

The hatch opened and the two of them began their descent inside. Sentry locked the latch behind him. Once they came to the bottom, Sentry could see a large bunker built to withstand any attack. It had thick metal walls with bolts running down the middle of different panels. Large metal beams were placed in the center for support. Further back, there was a large kitchen area with chrome counters and a rolling cart. Everything was chrome plated or stainless steel.

Sentry let out a whistle. "Wow, this place is impressive."

"I think my family never really trusted the Oculus. They always knew that one day they would need to get out or flee if it came to it." Antonia looked around. "Then, when my parents got sick, my father told me about this place and how to get here."

"Is that what made you want to leave? Them passing away?"

"No, I mean, I never wanted to join. But I was forced into it by the Oculus. They said that their members are in for life, and that means their children. My parents *had* to bring me into the fold."

"What did your parents do for the Oculus?"

"We're a legitimate energy company. We aren't corrupt like the Oculus, but my father told me that they forced them to join. I don't know exactly how. He never told me. But my parents gave their facilities and bases power so that they could keep their secret locations unknown from the world."

"Ah, that makes sense." Sentry let out a long sigh. "I wonder what made them stay."

"Whatever they used to force my parents to join, I suppose. Maybe it was their lives. But I don't know. Either way, my parents built this place, and they made their plans to escape or hide away here if the situation ever presented itself. But they got sick and they passed away before they were able to."

Sentry's lips formed a hard line, but his eyes looked softly at her. "I'm sorry about that. That must have been hard."

"It was. Until they told me about this place. Then everything became about preparing for my escape. Like I said, I never wanted this. I never wanted to be forced to work for this corrupt secret society. I just wanted to be a normal person. But I was never given that chance. Not until they told me about this place. My father told me that there was a key here to bringing down the Oculus." By the end, tears welled up in her eyes.

"Really?" asked Sentry. "What is it?"

She grew colder. "He said it was a secret. That he couldn't tell me just yet."

"What, why not?"

She looked around again, as if the walls were listening to them and then she looked back at Sentry. "He believed that we were being watched. That the Oculus was actually keeping an eye on us. So, he never told me." She laughed a little. "It's funny actually. How he told me just about this place."

"How did he tell you about it?"

"He would make little riddles and word puzzles for me to solve. I think he did that so that he could hide the information and make it look innocent. That way, no one but me could solve it."

"How did you solve them?"

"We have always loved puzzles. We even made up our own pigeon."

Sentry raised an eyebrow. "You made up a bird?"

"Pigeon is a blend of two languages. My family had a blend of Greek and Italian. Italian was my mother's language. We spoke both languages at home, and eventually we blended them together so we could communicate using our special blended language."

"So, he left you clues and puzzles in this hidden language so no one else could solve it?"

She nodded. "But he never left me the final clue. The final puzzle, he died before I could solve it."

A PLAN FOR REVENGE

They stood in the empty silence for some time. Due to the awkwardness hanging in the air, Sentry didn't know what to say. *Should I try to console her, or should I move on with the subject?* Shifting his weight from foot to foot, he looked over at her.

She didn't have tears in her eyes now. Instead, she looked stoic and unmoving, like a Greek statue with her jaw set. "But we still have a chance to make his death mean something."

Sentry nodded. "We will. Together, we'll bring down the Oculus and make them pay."

Antonia looked around the room as if this was her kingdom. "Well, let's go find my inheritance."

The two walked down the hallway and peeked into the different rooms. First, they passed what looked like a store room. There were barrels and boxes full of supplies, shelves were lined with canned goods, and a deep freezer that was still in the wrappings, had been pushed up against the wall. Then they passed a bedroom that was bigger than he'd expected to see down here. There were several beds. *In case Antonia has guests,* he assumed. There were a few other closed off rooms, but Sentry didn't ask what they were for. Finally, they came to the end of the bunker. Antonia opened the door and found herself looking into her father's study.

"Wow," Sentry said, looking into the room. "What is this place?"

"This is where my father collected all of his secrets against the Oculus." She pointed to the large server on the wall. "There's a secure network here. And there's his map."

The room had a massive map with pins in it. Sentry walked over to the map and scanned it. There were green pins, red pins, yellow pins, and more. He tried to find a pattern, but he didn't understand it. "So, what are these?"

Antonia pointed as she said, "They are different events from across the world. Some are Oculus attacks, some are locations of Oculus hideouts. He tracked all of the different dealings the Oculus had around the world to help him in his revenge."

"Is this what he left you then?"

"No, I don't think so. I think this was just for research. I never got the final puzzle, remember? So, we need to find the final clue and solve the mystery."

"Let's get moving then."

The two of them began looking through the room for the final piece of the puzzle, starting with her father's desk. There was a large tome of a notebook sitting on the desk. Leather-bound and dusty, the book seemed to house his notes. Antonia flipped through the pages as Sentry looked over her shoulder. All it seemed to be were schematics for his power plants.

"Well, this isn't helpful. Wonder what these power plant schemes are all about." Antonia brushed the book aside and continued to rifle through the desk for any other obvious clues. While she did that, Sentry found his way over to a bookcase and began looking through some of the books. There was a large collection of different mythology books. He had books on mythologies from all different cultures. There were old Norse myths, ancient Indian myths, Babylonian fables, Celtic fairy tales, and obviously Greek legends.

"Wow, your dad was a mythology buff, huh?" Sentry said.

"Oh yeah, he read me all those old tales when I was a kid."

Antonia didn't find much on the desk other than an odd collection of stamps, some fancy pens, and his calendar. Grabbing the calendar, thinking that might be the clue, she looked through it. He had drawn a heart around her birthday and written, "You have the power to do anything, Little Zapper."

Tears welled in her eyes as she read that and ran her fingers over the words. That was her father's nickname for her. No one else called her that. No one else even knew that nickname. How she longed to hear someone call her that again. Even just once.

She put the calendar down and wiped the tears from her eyes. She glanced over at Sentry to see if he'd noticed. He was standing feet away with his head in a book. She picked the calendar back up and continued to flip through it. Aside from a few odd birthdays and holidays, there was nothing of importance in it. She dropped it, grunting in frustration. Then she rescanned the desk.

Antonia pulled everything off of the desk and stacked it in a pile. Maybe there was something she overlooked. The top drawer was empty aside from a few pens. The second drawer had some notebooks and a tablet, but not much else.

She tapped her foot as she stood back up. Her mind was racing with thoughts, but nothing really was clicking. There had to be something here that she was missing. This had to be where the clue was. She was certain of it.

Sentry looked up from the mythology book he was reading. "You know I was just reading about all of the powers Zeus had. It made me wonder about your dad. Was your father gifted?"

"Yes, he was a very powerful gifted. He could generate energy with his lightning gift."

"Oh really?" Sentry asked. "Interesting, just like Zeus."

"Yeah, so?" Antonia asked.

Sentry placed a hand under his chin and sighed "Is that what made him go into the energy business?"

"Well, yeah. He was so powerful that he was able to run whole business and towns with his energy production. I heard he powered his whole town by himself." Then something clicked in her mind. "Wait!"

After finding the book in one of the stacks on the floor, she slammed the massive leather book on the desk. "The book with the power plant plans?" asked Sentry.

"Yes, I think *this* is what my father wanted me to find," she said.

"What do you mean?"

"Remember what I told you? My father was tasked with giving power to all of the Oculus bases and headquarters around the world. But if he wanted to get revenge on them and bring them down, what better way to do that than cut their power?"

Sentry's eyes widened. He leaned in as she thumbed through the book and studying the pages more thoroughly than before. Now that she knew what to look for, she was certain this would be the key. There were plans and schematics for gifted-based energy plants, high-efficiency generators, and power cell plans.

"What are these places?" asked Sentry.

Antonia was used to studying these kinds of blueprints since she was the CEO of the Sagas Corporation. The mechanical breakdowns, building dimensions as well as specifications of the layouts were noted on each page. Each building was unique. She kept cycling through the pages until she finally stopped on a separate section.

"These are the Oculus bases," she said. "See this one here? It says this is a base in San Julio. This one is off the coast of New Zealand."

Turning the pages, they stopped when they saw a strange building. No, it wasn't a building. It was a pyramid, more intricate and more ornate than the other layouts. It was located in the land of Pharaohs—Cairo, Egypt.

"Look at that one," Sentry said. "I've never seen a modern building like that."

"Few exist. This building is…hmm." The large blueprints were thick and durable, which was good with how intently Antonia was studying them. "I think…I think I understand now."

"What is it?" Sentry leaned in.

"The way he would get his final revenge. My father put in a failsafe. He made the buildings that fed off his power plants susceptible to a massive power shortage. Whenever he planned to take them down, he put this failsafe measure in place so that all of their bases could be cut off."

"You mean, we can pull the plug on every Oculus base at once?" Sentry's eyes widened.

"Yes, and in doing so, we cripple the Oculus once and for all."

Sentry smiled. "Great! How do we do it?"

"We need to get to this pyramid," she said, pointing to it.

Both of them stared down at the page. A daunting task lay before them. One that would've been impossible if they hadn't found these plans. They had to try. If they could even partially succeed, they could set the Oculus back years. Maybe decades.

"I'm in," he said.

"All right, we need to get a transport to Egypt, and then we need to sneak into this pyramid facility," she said.

Sentry looked intently. "Do you know of a transport?"

"There's a shipwright I know. He travels through here, and we could get passage on his cruise ship."

"All right. Will he take us to Egypt?"

DEATH ON A CRUISE SHIP

Fortunately, the two of them were able to get onto the transport with no trouble at all. The ship picked them up within the hour, and they were off. Aboard the ship, a steward showed them

to their rooms. It was a much fancier ship than Sentry had expected, but he'd forgotten he was traveling with the heiress of the Sagas fortune. This wasn't the ship you'd take for a regular family vacation. It was ornamented with beautiful wood engravings and marble statues.

In their room, Sentry was surprised to see how spacious it was. The only other cruise he'd been on had been much more cramped. The large room was the maybe double size of his apartment back home. "Is this a special room or something?"

"It's the Queen's Suite. It's for some of the most important passengers."

"Wow, this is impressive," he said, looking at the bronze sconces on the wall.

"Well, make yourself at home. We should be in Egypt tomorrow."

"I guess I'll head to sleep then." Sentry turned.

"No chance. We are going to get some dinner."

Sentry didn't know what to say. She just stood there, tapping her foot again. He looked back as if someone was coming to save him, but there was no one there, and he was in over his head. She shrugged, palms up.

"But you need to stay safe. I need to protect you."

"Well, I'm going to get some dinner so if you want to protect me, you'll need to come to dinner as well."

He rolled his eyes. "Fine."

A few minutes later, a tailor was in the room fitting Sentry for a new charcoal gray suit with a green shirt. He looked in the mirror as the tailor cleaned everything up and actually found himself impressed by the fit and how well the color complimented his complexion and eye color. Then he turned around. Antonia was a cream-colored dress.

She held her arm out. "Well?"

He raised an eyebrow. "What?"

"My arm. Aren't you going to take it?"

"Oh, okay." He moved and put his arm out for her to take. The two of them walked out of their lavish suite and down to the dining hall.

As they walked in, Sentry looked over his shoulder. He thought he sensed something and pushed out with his TK radar, but it was gone.

Antonia pulled him along. "What's wrong?" she whispered through a false smile.

"I thought I sensed something. Like a telekinetic pressure."

"Don't be silly. It must have just been a worker or maybe a performer," she said. "Now, let's go in an enjoy some dinner for a change."

Sentry found himself floored by the exquisite decor and the over-the-top luxury of it all. The extravagant red carpet and the white China plates made for a beautiful atmosphere, though. Servers in white suits appeared to pull out their chairs and take their drink orders. They were back in a matter of seconds.

"Man, this is living," Sentry joked.

"It is for some people," she said in a flat tone.

Sentry couldn't tell if she missed it, or if she was over the lavish and decadent lifestyle. He wondered for a moment. Then he noticed something over her shoulder. For a split second, he thought that the person was watching them. When he started watching, the man went back to his dinner and never looked back up. But it seemed odd. *Is he actually watching us, or was it just a coincidence?* he wondered.

They were given courses served on delicate white China with gold filigree. Small flower petals decorated the centers of each dish. But as wonderful as the dinner was, Sentry's defenses were up now. At one point, he dropped a fork. As he bent down to grab it, he did a quick scan of the room. Then, after the third course, he got up to ask a waiter for a napkin. This time when he scanned the room, he noticed a woman walking past the table that looked to be watching them. She passed quickly, and the glance was only momentary.

He sat back down, and he looked at Antonia. "Hey, I just want you to be aware. I think we may be being watched."

"You do know I'm something of a celebrity in Europe, right?" she said. "Maybe they're just looking at me and being star struck."

"I mean, no, I didn't realize that. But I've seen at least two people looking at us."

"That's it?" she asked. "Two? I'm surprised it's not more actually."

"Well, uh, I guess…" He trailed off, unsure of what to say.

"Just enjoy the dinner. Tomorrow we will be back to chasing super villains and fighting off evil robots." She laughed.

He tried to laugh it off, but he still wasn't sure. Maybe he was being paranoid, but he didn't want to let his guard down. He would rather be paranoid and wrong, than be self-assured and dead. It might have seemed extreme, but in that moment, that was how he felt. It was really as black and white as that. The Oculus's reach was so vast that any one of these people could be an associate, an assassin, or even just an informant. Regardless, they weren't as safe as Antonia wanted to believe.

The fifth course, which was the main meal, was a medium-rare piece of steak, and it had some fancy name that Sentry couldn't remember, but it was exquisite. He enjoyed each bite. Then they received a dessert. Sentry had the New York-style cheesecake, his absolute favorite. It was served with a strawberry glaze on the side. That was enough to make him want to call it a day then and there, but then they brought out another desert.

"What's this?" Sentry asked, looking at the dessert on his plate.

"It's the mignardise," she explained.

"What does that even mean?"

"It's kind of like a bite-sized treat. It's a chocolate tart."

"But we already got our dessert."

She laughed. "Yes, I know. It's the finale of the meal. Go ahead and try it."

He took a bite and fell back in an exaggerated faint. "What in the world...That was amazing. Why didn't they just serve that for the dessert?"

"It's a little show for the chefs. They aren't always part of the meal, but it's served for special occasions and such." She sipped her decaf coffee.

"That might have been the fanciest meal I've ever eaten," he said.

"Good I'm glad. Why don't we walk about the deck. Get some air and walk off some of this food?"

"Sure." He moved to her side and helped her up and then he extended his arm, looking over his shoulder once more to see if anyone else was coming up behind them. No one else left at the same time, but he wasn't sure they were safe just yet.

Above deck, they found themselves under a starlit sky. The night air was cool but enjoyable. Sentry undid his collar now that they were out of the fancy dining hall. They turned, went around the back of the ship, and kept walking. They saw a few dolphins swimming and jumping through the moonlit sky.

As they walked around the bow of the ship, the crowds began to thin. When they made a second loop, still talking and enjoying the calm evening air, they realized they were some of the only people on deck. *Is it getting late?* He checked his watch, but it was only about nine in the evening, so he was surprised at how few people were out.

A large black cloud blotted out the bright moon, and everything darkened. Then a heavy rain started. The last of the passengers immediately rushed off the deck disappeared. Sentry looked over to Antonia and nodded. She shook her head.

He laughed. "You want to stay out here?"

"Just for a minute. I haven't done anything normal in so long, I just want to enjoy the beauty of the night for a minute," she said, her beautiful evening gown already soaked.

But then the lightning started. A bolt came down close to the boat, but the crack of thunder was even more alarming. Sentry found the sound disorienting.

At that moment, Titus rushed out with a surge of telekinetic energy. He slammed into Sentry, pressing down hard. Pushing back against the power of his opponent's telekinesis, Sentry stood up.

"Nice try, but our powers practically cancel each other out."

Titus smirked. "That's why I brought friends."

Three of his goons came out of nowhere. The first two rushed at them, while the other stood back. Then the realization dawned on him. She was controlling the weather and needed to concentrate to help up the storm. Not only would it keep the passengers away, but it made the fight harder. The ship was now rocking back and forth and side to side. Sentry had the advantage of being able to use his telekinesis to steady himself, but so did Titus. If anything, he was even more practiced at this.

Sentry held out a hand so Antonia would remain in place. Walking forward, he took up a defensive stance. As the first goon came at him, the ship rocked again. Sentry stepped into the movement and was able to counter the attack. He threw the first attacker back into the second, sending them both into a spinning slide over the slick deck.

Then Titus rushed at him. He seemed mostly unfazed by the rocking, which gave Titus an edge. He moved easily, even when the boat lurched sharply to one side. Sentry was able to right himself each time it happened, but it took more of his concentration than it did for his enemy.

Because of Titus's condition, he was used to using his telekinesis to correct his posture and his movement. He had been using his gift to walk and move for years, so this was second nature to him. Sentry threw a punch that narrowly missed as the boat shifted quickly back to the right. Titus countered and sent him flying backwards.

He caught himself and got back up. *How am I going to take on three enemies at once when Titus alone is difficult enough?* He briefly looked back over at Antonia. She was standing with an arm out, but he didn't quite know what she was doing. Maybe she was trying to stand ready in case anyone came at her. Sentry shook his head. He wouldn't let anyone get close to her. He would need to think of something. Even if he had to bring everyone down with him, he wouldn't let them capture Antonia. She was the key to stopping the Oculus.

He pushed the first down with a telekinetic shove. The second, who seemed to be made of rubber, took all three of Sentry's hits with little to no effect. Then he punched with a fist that felt like being hit by a rubber band. It stung, but it wasn't too bad. Instead of fighting back, Sentry grabbed the rubber man's arm and kicked off him, stretching it out. Then he pulled and slammed him over his shoulder and onto the ground.

But Titus didn't let him get away with that. He attacked Sentry with reckless abandon, moving and swaying easily as the boat rocked up and down. He pushed Sentry back, causing him to slip and fall on the wet floor. But it wasn't enough to do more than slow Sentry down. Sentry then moved forward to engage with Titus, who was already back in motion. Sentry and Titus clashed as their telekinetic energy sparked and hissed between them. Sentry kicked off and sailed backwards, giving him some space.

The two goons rushed at him, which was what Sentry was hoping they'd do. By creating space, maybe he could fight all three. Sentry rushed at the foes ahead of him and engaged them. He kicked the first one in the ribs and then used a push of energy to drop him to the ground. Only TK attacks would work on the rubber man. The rubber man was already coming at him, so Sentry stepped back to dodge his attack, throwing a punch that rung his bell. Then he spun around and used another push of telekinesis that caused them to stumble forward, right toward Antonia.

Sentry's eyes widened as he realized what he had done. But something completely unexpected happened. He watched it all as if in slow motion. A crackle of energy sparked down her arm and a torrent of energy erupted from her palm. A brilliant beam of yellowish-orange plasma slammed into the first goon and the second. Both of them were blasted up and off of the side of the boat. Sentry turned to watch them fade away.

Then she held up her hand. A bolt of lightning came down and struck her. But instead of being shocked to death, she absorbed the bolt and more orange energy crackled around her. She held her hand out toward Titus. The crackle of energy around her intensified as the beam charged up. Then there was a flash as the beam erupted once again, slamming into Titus. He tried to shield himself from her attack, but the beam was too intense. His shield cracked. Then there was an explosion of telekinetic energy. The surge of energy was like a wave that sent everything around flying away. Ship equipment, some loose chairs, and a few tables all went flying in different directions. Even Titus's other goon was sent flying off the edge. As the beam connected with Titus, he was shot up into the air and sent flying backwards out of sight, over the edge and into the water.

Once Sentry dropped his own shield, he turned to Antonia and walked over with wide eyes. "What was that?"

She was staring at her hand in shock. "I've never done that before."

"The energy gift?"

"No, I've used my gift before. I mean, I've never used it like that. As a weapon."

Sentry nodded. "Right. It's strange, isn't it? Using something that can create and help the world, but having to hurt someone with it. I wish it wasn't like that."

"Me neither."

"But that was impressive."

She gave him a halfhearted smile. "Thank you. I come from a long line of powerful energy users so it comes in handy."

"I'll say. You made short work of those guys."

"Thanks, but it was hard to aim. That's why I made the blast so big. I figured why be accurate when I can just make it bigger?"

Sentry laughed again. "I guess that works."

"Let's get inside before someone sees us," he said. As they walked back toward the main deck, Sentry looked out over the water and pushed out his thoughts, hoping Serena might hear him and find them. Hopefully, they would be able to help.

FILE #17

UNDERCOVER

At the Oculus base, Marcus Pharis walked down the hall. He opened the door to his right and entered the large medical laboratory. At the far side of the room, Aria Guerrero was looking at a petri dish. She was up to her elbows in alchemical experiments again. Like usual, she was trying to find a cure for Titus's condition. Marcus thought it was probably hopeless, but he didn't really care in the end.

He walked over and cleared his throat. "Aria."

She held up a hand to signal that she needed another moment. Then she turned around and removed her gloves. "Yes, what is it?"

"You've done a lot for the Oculus. That is beyond question. Your medical research and creation of medicines have made the Oculus rich beyond question, thanks to our controlling stake in your pharmaceutical company."

"Yes, that's correct. Is there supposed to be a question in there?" she asked.

"And all of it was with the hope of creating a cure for your son, right?" he asked.

"Well, yes, that has always been my dream. I want desperately to help him. Give him some peace if I can. Every mother wants that for their children."

"But think of all you've accomplished! Your alchemical gift has allowed you to create hundreds of medicines that have cured so many diseases and helped so many people."

"Regardless, my goal is the same. Helping others is good, and the money is nice, but in the end, it all comes back down to helping find something that will help Titus."

Just then, a guard came into the room. "Madam, we have some bad news."

"What's wrong?" she asked.

"My team has reports that we lost Titus last night. He never checked back in, and none of his team members are responding. We believe he was lost in a battle."

Aria's eyes widened. Marcus held out his arms to give her a hug. "Aria, I am so sorry."

She moved closer but didn't embrace him. She wasn't the emotional type. She just stood there. "How could this be?"

The guard looked down and then back up at her. "The last we heard from him was when he was tracking down Antonia Sagas. He told one of our operatives they were moving somewhere in Greece. However, he learned that she was being protected by an agent known as Sentry. All we know is that, ever since then, he and his team have been radio silent. We are starting to fear the worst."

Marcus pulled back when he saw Aria's expression. He had never seen a look so intense before. Normally, she was so timid, almost mouse-like, but she stood there with a fire in her eyes. Her jaw was tight, and he thought he saw her shaking. Then she turned to him and spoke. It almost made him jump.

"What do we need to do? Whatever you need from me, just let me know."

He nodded and smiled. "Of course."

A few minutes later, he walked out of her lab, returning to his own office, and sat behind his desk. He grabbed a water and drank from it, pulling in deep gulps. A guard came into the room. It was the same guard that had told Aria the bad news.

"How did I do, sir?" he asked.

Marcus smiled. "You did well. Thank you again for being the bearer of bad news. But it was better that way."

"Thank you, sir. Why did you want me to tell her when you were the one who informed me?" the guard asked with a quizzical look on his face.

"I needed to speak with her about upcoming plans, and I didn't want her decision to be clouded by that, so I found a third party to be the best way to inform her of the situation with her son."

"Oh, okay, sir. Anything else?"

"No, that will be all."

The guard turned and left. Marcus sat in his office alone for some time. He smiled. Everything was moving smoothly. He now had Aria firmly in his corner. He was positioning himself nicely, and it would be good to have someone like Aria on his side. He wanted to make a play at bringing Jules over to his side as well, but he would need to tread carefully there. She was loyal to Zeno due to his help in pushing her agency up in the Protectorate.

He needed to make sure he handled that tactfully. He was rather adept at handling difficult negotiations in his business, but he wanted to make sure he could save face if she didn't want to work with him. At that thought, Marcus sat forward at his desk. He clasped his hands together and pondered the difficulty of their organization. In his time here, there were multiple factions that came and went over the years. Backstabbing was part of the game from his experience. Some were more overt, and those usually paid the price for it. Others were more tactful.

Marcus stood and looked out the window. *What would be the best way to convince Jules, or Lightbringer, as she was called in her agency?* He sighed deeply. It would have been so much easier to work with someone like Dexter Romulus. Yes, he was more loyal to the old man, but he would have seen the writing on the wall. At least, Marcus was pretty sure he would have. Then he started to pace. *What to do? What to do?*

Little did he know that Sentry and Antonia were in the city now. They had entered quietly that morning, and Antonia used her connections to get them escorted off of the cruise ship. Thanks to her clout, the ship's crew helped them leave with little to no one seeing them. The entourage brought them to a hotel, where they were immediately brought into the room without being seen. Then they were able to hide away and plan. It was fortunate, really, because Marcus and the Oculus had spies everywhere. Now they were on high alert. There were people looking for Antonia Sagas all over the world. Surely, they would have been seen.

"Well, we made it," Sentry said, putting down his small duffle bag. Antonia had purchased some clothes for him since all he had was his agency's three-piece suit. If he was going to play the part, he needed to look like a tourist.

"Indeed," she said. "Now what?"

Sentry smoothed his shirt. "I think tonight we try and sneak out to scout the area. We should try and be inconspicuous, so maybe we play it like we're going to dinner. Then we slip away and try and check out this pyramid."

"That's a good idea. So, we use the cover of night and pretend like we are just out on the town?"

"Pretty much."

"Well, we have several hours before then. What should we do with our time?"

"What does this hotel have in the way of spa and relaxation activities?" Sentry smiled.

Antonia nodded. "They have quite a few."

They spent the remainder of the morning and afternoon pampering themselves. They started with oatmeal scrub baths and then they each received a deep-tissue massage. The massage was a little too intense for Sentry's preferences, but afterwards he noticed that it did help with some of the aches and soreness he had been experiencing from days on the run. After that, Antonia and

Sentry met up for some lunch and discussed how their day had gone so far, which was enjoyable.

Sentry kept thinking about how unusual this all was. As an agent, most of the time, he didn't have time for the nice things. He was always on the run, going from mission to mission. And then when he wasn't on a mission, he found himself training. On the weeks in between assignments, he was in the gym multiple times a day. Then he would have medical examinations, physicals, reports to fill out, as well as the psychological evaluations. It was never ending. He sighed. It was so different in real life compared to the movies. In film, the spies were always driving fancy cars, visiting lavish destinations with fully inclusive suites. But in reality, the life of a secret agent was somewhat overwhelming.

After lunch, they walked over to the spa area again. "Oh, look, they have a spa treatment that is 'highly recommended for the overstressed gifted,'" Antonia said, reading a sign.

"What does that mean?"

"I'm not sure, but it might be worth a look."

"I don't know…"

"Oh, come on." Antonia dragged him down to the next spa area and practically pushed him into the room. Inside, there was a woman standing on a large carpet. She waved him inside.

"So, what is this spa treatment?" asked Sentry.

"It's a sensory deprivation tank. Inside, you will be removed almost entirely from any and all sensations. You'll feel like you're in a void of nothingness."

"And this is supposed to help me with my gift?" He was almost indignant.

The woman smiled in an overly sweet way. "Actually, yes. We have found that this treatment is remarkably effective amongst gifted. Studies have shown that there is a link in gifted performances and stress. By helping remove all of our senses, we have found that one can increase their connection to their gift."

"Well, if there's a chance this'll help me out, I'll take it. I'm in."

"Very good," She escorted him to another room. Here everything was very dimly lit. There were a few large, black chambers. She pressed a button on one of them and the pod opened up to reveal water inside. Sentry looked around and saw a few of the pods were blinking with a red light marked Occupied.

"Here, you will enter the pod and there you will remain for the next hour. In that time, you'll be able to experience the full benefits of the sensory deprivation pod."

Sentry was then allowed to put on a pair of swim trunks before he entered the pod. He put on a small breathing mask and laid in the water. At first, it was strange and almost unsettling. The lack of sense, the weightlessness, and the inability to tell what was happening around him. Then he experienced the deafness. At first, it was just quiet, but then the silence was almost overwhelming. But then he started to relax and regulating his breath. He calmed his mind and that was when things went from strange to relaxing.

For the next hour, Sentry relaxed in the pod with little to no awareness of the world around him. In the end, he experienced a place of complete relaxation. He found the experience unusual, but it was also completely freeing. When the woman opened the pod to let him out, he almost wanted to ask her if he could stay in there for another hour or even two.

He left the relaxation chamber, feeling completely at peace, which was good because the next step of their plan was the most dangerous yet. They would be heading into the belly of the beast—enemy territory.

FILE #18

THE PYRAMID

That evening, the pair began the next step in their plan. Once it was dark, they dressed for the part. Sentry used his agency suit, just in case they were caught up in a fight. In their room, they got ready and ordered a driver to take them down to a restaurant. They chose a fairly normal place to eat, nothing too fancy or over the top. The plan was to stay under the radar. They arrived, doing their best to seem unassuming. Antonia wore a pair of oversized sunglasses and had done her makeup differently.

After they were seated and their food had been served, they ate in almost complete silence. Through the entire meal, Sentry was looking over his shoulder, even though he was sitting in the back so he could face the door. Although he felt good after his spa day, he was anxious for what they would find next. After they finished eating, Sentry practically jumped out of his seat.

"All right, let's move," he said.

"Are you actually excited by the prospect of going into an enemy base and maybe dying?" Antonia asked him.

Sentry smirked. "Maybe a little."

She rolled her eyes and laughed. "All right, let's go."

The two exited the building and found their driver. They had the driver bring them to a park near the pyramid. There they were able to get out and then walk the perimeter. As they walked down the sidewalk of the park, the pyramid was to their left. Sentry did a scan around them with his eyes to see if anyone around them was acting like some kind of lookout. It was times like these he wished he had his team with him. Insight would be able to pick out a lookout in seconds, Brimstone would have helped them in a fight, and Codex would be able to get them into and out of the pyramid without their security having any idea they were ever there.

Like he did on the boat, Sentry looked out into the distance and thought once again of his team, pushing out his mind to call to them. Maybe Insight would be close enough to track them. He didn't know where they were, if they were together, or if they were captured. He hoped he had made the right call by taking Antonia and getting out of dodge. He hoped he was right not to leave a trail for them to follow because he didn't know who he could trust or if the Oculus would find them. But he didn't have time to dwell on that now. He was on the lookout. They were about to embark on a dangerous mission.

He turned back to Antonia. "Looks like the perimeter is clear. I don't see any lookouts."

"That's good."

"Let's move closer."

At first, they had been keeping a wide berth. They didn't want to dive in with no plan of escape. Now that the perimeter was pretty clear, they would be able to get closer. Sentry and Antonia kept walking, doing their best to appear like a couple on a leisurely stroll in the park, until just ahead of them was the pyramid. The large wall around it was a unique design, made to look like it had ancient Egyptian hieroglyphics on it. The building itself was strange as well. Although it was a pyramid, it was built to look almost futuristic. There were mechanical patterns down the sides and portions that were actually windows, but blacked out so they couldn't be spied on.

"See those windows?" Sentry asked. "That'll make it hard to see much." Antonia sighed.

The pyramid was on the far edge of the city. There're weren't other buildings near it, which was unfortunate because their cover was no longer going to be usable. Now that they were coming into the large area near the pyramid, they would need to be on their guard. They left the park and crossed the street, both running down into the open field. There were lots of rocky outcroppings, and in the distance, they could see a large hill. Sentry pointed it out, and they both turned that direction.

They dropped down behind it, and Sentry pushed out with his senses. He began scanning to pick up any lifeforms or unusual things nearby. After a few moments, he turned to Antonia. "I think we're in the clear."

They moved up the hill, keeping as low to the ground as possible. The loose rocks and sand made it somewhat difficult to move up the hillside, but once they crested the top of the hill, they could once again see the pyramid. With the sun gone, everything was cast in shadow, everything except what was directly under the huge lights. In between them and the pyramid was a rocky field with nothing but hilly outcroppings and areas of grass scattered in patches here and there.

"We can't exactly make a quick break for it, so we need to figure out a way to get closer," said Sentry.

"Before we bother getting closer, I need to determine where the power conduit is."

Sentry looked over at her. "Oh, that's a good point. So, like, you know how to take out the power and everything right?"

"Of course. I figured that out after a few minutes of looking at the schematics."

"Really?"

Antonia smiled. "Yeah, it's pretty simple, really. I'm going to just overload the conduit, and that should kill the reactor so that the power to the other bases and sites is cut."

"How are you going to do that?" he asked.

"I just need to blast it.

"Oh, okay. I thought it was going to be a little more technical than that. You know, maybe crack a firewall, break into a circuit, overload the breakers, something like that."

"Nope. Honestly, if I could determine exactly which corner was the right one, I would take a shot from here. But without knowing I'm hitting the right area, I don't want to take a shot at it. I might only have one chance at this."

Sentry nodded. "All right then."

He turned to look at the pyramid. Personally, he had no idea what he was seeing. Sentry wasn't trained in architecture or engineering, so the entire thing was a question mark for him. All he knew was that he needed to protect Antonia so she could figure out what to do next. Antonia pulled out the schematics from before and began to look over the specifics. Sentry looked over, trying to help. He could see lines and numbers, but he couldn't make heads or tails of it.

"Are those measurements?" he asked

"No, these are over here."

"Oh, okay. What about that?"

"This is the power main," she said.

The two of them both had their heads down looking down on the page. Sentry was pointing to one point, but Antonia was shaking her head. They were both so engaged in the schematics, that neither of them saw what was coming up behind them. There was a shadow that loomed ever closer. Sentry noticed it first. He stood and instantly flared his telekinetic energy. It pulsed around him, but then he saw what it was. A whole team of guards had snuck up behind them.

Before him stood seven or eight guards in dark green camouflage cargos and black shirts. Each of them was standing with fists ready to fight. Then one of them dropped his fighting stance and stepped forward. "Agent Sentry, I presume?" he asked.

"Who wants to know?" asked Sentry.

"My employer would like to welcome you two into the building. Ms. Sagas, we would like to accompany you as well."

Sentry looked around for a moment. One on eight was not a fight he wanted to undertake, even in a normal situation, and especially not with Antonia here. True she could put out a lot of energy with her gift. But could she stand in a fight with eight well trained and probably very powerful guards? Everything inside him railed against the idea of giving up and going with them. It took more self-control then he through he had inside of him. Maybe it was maturity. Maybe this was growing up. A few years ago, if he had been in this same situation, Sentry knew he would probably have gone down swinging. He would have fought them and probably died trying.

He looked over at Antonia, who looked frightened. She probably had no experience with these intense types of negotiations. He couldn't put her in a situation where she would be killed. Sentry sighed and looked over at the guard. "All right, we'll come quietly. But if you make one move to hurt her, I'll turn on you."

"You really think you can take all of us?" asked the guard to his right. She was a tall woman with a scar on her chin.

"No, but I bet I could bring a few of you down. And guess which one of you I am taking out first." He glaring at her with a fire in his eyes.

The guards parted and Antonia walked through them with Sentry on her heels. He made sure he was right beside her as they trekked down the hillside and over the patchy field. The whole time the two of them kept looking over at each other. Antonia tried to reassure him with her gaze, while Sentry was trying to do the same for her. She gave him a nod and he nodded back. Together they walked down into the unknown. They were now in the belly of the beast. Sentry knew of the danger ahead of him, but he wasn't sure that he could protect her.

Meanwhile, inside Antonia was smiling.

I have him exactly where I want him.

She gave him a shy smile, hoping that it would put him at ease. She felt bad for getting him caught up in this, but she needed his help. If nothing else, he had done his part. But in the end, she would have her revenge. Bringing her inside the pyramid was

Bartholomew Zeno's biggest mistake so far. She was just that much closer to her goal. It only made her job easier. Zeno just didn't realize it.

A jeep drove up beside them. It was large with a flatbed for a trunk. He guards all ushered Sentry and Antonia into the back. They filed in behind them, cramming into the space. Sentry was in between Antonia and a huge man. He probably needed his own aisle for himself. His muscled arms kept bumping into Sentry as they drove. He pushed him a little to make room, but the guard didn't budge.

The gates ahead of them opened, and they could see the entrance to the pyramid just ahead of them. Now it was real. They were really here. Nothing could prepare them for the welcome they would receive. Sentry was wondering what kind of tortures or evil plans were waiting for him inside. Then he thought about what they would do to Antonia. But no amount of thinking could have prepared him for what was waiting for him. Nothing.

FILE #19

NEGOTIATIONS

They were brought into a large hanger. It was like a massive garage, with tons of vehicles. For whatever reason, the Oculus looked like it was prepared for any situation—military assault, underwater excursion, hunting in the wilderness, you name it, and they were ready for it. They had robotics gear as well as crates containing different gear for a computer lab. It looked like they had just received a new shipment. Sentry wasn't sure if this was all brand new, or if these materials were always here just in case.

Once the jeep stopped, the two of them were escorted out of the vehicle. Sentry tried to prepare himself for what came next. Despite himself, he tried to push the thoughts of possibly being brought to a torture chamber from his mind. Part of him thought thinking of it might better prepare him for the eventuality. But instead of a torture chamber, they turned and brought them into a large open room that was decorated like a lavish throne room. There were garish chairs made of dark, rich woods that rested on top of lush, wide carpets.

"What is this place?" Sentry looked around, expecting something to come out of every corner to kill them.

"This is where we meet all of our guests," said a voice from behind the wall. Then a hidden door in the wall opened to reveal the one-person Sentry never expected to see again.

Bartholomew Zeno stood before them dressed in a white three-piece suit with black buttons and a black tie. He smiled, which made his wrinkled, old face crease with lines. Brushing the thinning hairs on his head back, he stopped a few feet in front of them.

He put his hands out to encompass the room. "It's actually a pretty interesting room. Let me show you." He waved for them to follow as he moved over to a showcase-sized display case. It was massive, like what you might see in the lobby of a high school where they show off their division titles and honors award winners. Inside the case were several unique relics.

"This is one of my favorite pieces, an ancient Egyptian hieroglyphic," he said, pointing to a stone piece. It was hanging on the wall on a stand. The hieroglyphics were somewhat faded from time, but they were remarkably well preserved for something that he was claiming to be ancient. "These hieroglyphics actually tell of a large meteor that struck the land thousands of years ago. They speak of a strange green stone. Here. See?"

Sentry leaned in and he could see some of the pictures were more obvious than others. He pointed to one. "Hmm, interesting."

"My scientists believe this meteor was the first time venisium landed on Earth." Then he moved over to the center of the display and pointed again to another artifact. This one was a piece of broken, twisted rock.

"What's that?"

"This is that very meteorite. We have studied it extensively, and it is most definitely from Venus. My scientists are certain of it," Bartholomew Zeno said.

Sentry leaned closer to study it. It reminded him of the large meteor he and his team went to secure. The very same one that started all of this. He let out a long, drawn out sigh.

"Not impressed?" Bartholomew raised an eyebrow.

"No, it's impressive all right. But, it just makes me think. I wonder why we put so much stock in all of this power. If you ask me, it's more trouble than it's worth."

"Maybe to those without the vision and forethought to see the potential." Zeno crossed his arms.

"Yeah, I'm sure you have all of the insight in the world. But in my experience, trying to attain and hold onto all of this power just creates more problems. Sure you have power and wealth and everything, but what do you lose when you're so focused on holding onto that power?" Sentry finally turned to look Zeno in the eyes.

Zeno took a step back and nodded. "Yes, fair point. If not somewhat naive."

Naive, Sentry thought. *That word is used to describe me a lot...* By his professors, his instructors at the Academy, his superiors, and even the Protectorate itself. Sure it wasn't always the exact word, sometimes it was a more subtle term, like innocent, young, or sincere. Other times they were more direct, more pointed. Some called him ignorant or foolish, even. A few used the term uncultured or unsophisticated.

Regardless of how they said it, they all meant the same thing. They thought he was naive. They thought he was foolish for wanting a world that was peaceful and kind. Maybe he was. Maybe it was an impossible dream to try and see the good in people. But that was the world Sentry found himself still longing for.

"Maybe," he said. "Maybe I am naive. But if you offered me all of the power in the world, and I knew what I do now—about how you have to fight, and kill, and lie to keep it all—I would tell you to take it back. I don't want it."

Zeno shook his head. "You are an interesting case, Mr. Green."

Something about how he said that. About how he called him by his name was alarming to Sentry. It reminded him that this wasn't like the villains he faced in the past. This wasn't some faceless goon with power and that was it. Zeno knew Sentry, probably had known of him for years even before he got to the Academy, and now, he was here with all of the cards in his hand. He had stacked the deck against Sentry, and he had every possibility in front of him. He knew Sentry's friends, family, and his team. He could do anything he wanted because he had every single advantage.

"You aren't like the other agents I have used in the past. You are more starry-eyed than most. But I think that offers a unique potential. Unlike the others that want something simple. Like power or money for example. Those things make it so simple really. But not you. You are a visionary. You see the way the world could be. Like me."

Sentry's stomach dropped into his toes and his veins flooded with ice at those words. Never in all of his wildest dreams would he have thought that Zeno and he were anything alike. Bartholomew was a respected member of the Protectorate, who was actually some kind of super-secret villain with a secret base. Sentry was just a kid who wanted to help the world, which was why he had become an agent. Now, he was on the run and had nothing to show for it. Nothing but a failed mission and a group of lost friends.

"How do you figure you and I are alike?" he asked, shifting his body so his hips and legs were somewhat tilted. He crossed his arms.

"Like I said, you are a visionary. Like me and like everyone else in the Oculus. We are all devoted to making this world better, one way or another."

"Really, that's your goal? What about the killing, stealing, and destruction we've seen over the last few years? All of it, I believe, was at the hands of the Oculus."

"Sentry—oh excuse me. Gabriel," he corrected. "Have you heard the expression, 'Rome wasn't built in a day'?"

Sentry didn't speak. He just nodded.

"Well, we all believe. No, we know we can't change the world in a day. We are committed to making it better. But in some cases, you have to get your hands dirty. You have to do things you might not enjoy. Maybe you have to even kill to see the world changed and improved in the end."

Sentry shook his head. "How? How can you justify a world that is built off of blood and death?"

Zeno nodded and turned to look at the display case, scanning from left to right. "You know, I understand you concern. I've wrestled with that question for years. Because of my gift, I have lived to see several generations. Living so long makes one see the world in a different light. You don't just see your single, solitary life. You see the bigger picture. You see the beginning and the middle, and you can start to see the end. That's where I want to get the world. If I can push the world a little more, they will be ready to accept the changes that Oculus wants to make. We want to see everything united and prosperous. But we need to make the world accept that."

Sentry grit his teeth. "You just have to kill a few hundred more people to get the world to believe in your new world."

Zeno nodded and faced him. "If that is what it takes. Then so be it."

Antonia was standing quietly as Zeno spoke. Even though Sentry wasn't a telepath like Insight, he could tell she was doing everything she could to keep her anger in check. He saw the tight jaw, the eyes darting left and right, the white-knuckled fist that she kept rotating. Then he turned back to Zeno. But before he could speak, Zeno interjected.

"I want to offer you and Antonia a proposition. Join us. Join the Oculus and we will work together. We will concede to being more—" He paused, thinking of the word. "*Humane* in our approaches. We'll make every effort to refrain from more overt shows of force. But we will require more from you as well."

"No deal," Sentry said, not even waiting to hear the other end of the bargain.

"Wait until you hear both sides of the proposition, Sentry."

"I don't need to. I'm not working with you."

Not being one to turn away from a hard bargain, Zeno snapped his fingers. Immediately, six guards popped out of nowhere. They just materialized into the room. "You know what. You are tired, and you aren't thinking clearing. Why don't you take the next few hours to rest?"

The guards moved in and started pushing Sentry and Antonia toward the other door. As they did, Sentry looked over to Zeno. Zeno readjusted his jacket. "We will speak again tonight at dinner."

FILE #20

PRISONERS

As they walked out, Antonia was practically seething with rage. It took every ounce of her self-control to not unleash her gift on Zeno right then and there. The only thing that kept her in check was the realization that Zeno wasn't as unprotected as it seemed. Someone was either in the room unseen and hidden, or they were using their gifts. The fact that those guards had been teleported into the room without anyone in the room was proof of that.

The guards turned down a long, dark hallway. Bronze sconces on the wall offered dim light. Antonia didn't know this area. It wasn't the area where they usually met. Or at least she didn't think so. She was only ever here when they summoned her for meetings, but she needed to figure out the layout soon.

If she could just get close. Maybe not even close, but just on the same floor as the reactor. Then she could just unleash every ounce of her power to destroy it. That was all she needed. *Maybe I should just blast away and take the whole building down.* That was it, she would just explode all of her energy and bring the building down on herself and Zeno. But then she thought about that more thoroughly. From her estimations of the schematics, the building was designed in a way that there could be several walls in between her and the reactor. Maybe it wouldn't be as doable as she originally believed.

Then they went into the holding rooms. At first, Antonia was expecting a prison cell, but when she was ushered inside, she realized it was more like a hotel room. The room was a sterile white color with little to no decor. The sparse pieces in the room were all chrome and angular. As she glanced at a lamp and then a small end table, she realized that both were bolted down. Maybe it was more of a prison cell after all.

Sentry was pushed into an almost identical one. He scanned the room for anything unusual. Along with the lack of any personality, the room was rather safe. Well, as safe as it could be for being a holding cell in a base where a secret society of gifted individuals worked. There was a white spherical device on the wall in the corner. He nodded at it, realizing that it was almost definitely a camera. Now the only question was, did the camera have audio as well? That might dictate his next move.

He circled the room, popping his head into the restroom, touching the small end table, and even hopping onto the bed. Everything seemed normal, and there weren't any other obvious cameras. However, his main purpose in moving around the room was to see if the camera moved. As he moved to the far side of the room, he noticed that the spherical device moved and spun. His best guess was that the camera had a pretty good range, which meant anywhere he went in the room was probably being tracked by the security team.

I wonder if I could reach out to Codex, he thought as he looked at the television that was bolted to the wall. *I miss my team…Maybe I was stupid for going off on my own.*

Then something came to him. He laid back down on the bed, looked up at the ceiling, and started putting together the bare bones pieces of a plan. Maybe even that was being generous. But in time, he would have an idea. He needed to have an idea. One way or another, he would figure out what they needed to do next. It took him a few hours of sitting in the room, pacing, and then finally sitting back down. But in the end, he was pretty certain he had come up with a plan.

On another floor, while walking with purpose, Marcus Pharis ran into some of the guards that had just escorted Sentry to the holding room. He turned to them, unsure as to why there were so many of the guards clumped up together. "Is everything all right?"

"Oh, yessir," said one of the guards in a thick British accent. "Just escorted two prisoners to the holding rooms."

"Prisoners?" Marcus stepped back.

"Yes, that agent, Sentry, and Antonia were both apprehended."

Marcus wanted to yell, but he caught himself. His reaction was to ask if this was serious. But he couldn't let any of that show. There were eyes everywhere. "Oh really?" he asked. "Well, I guess we will be deciding her fate soon. Nice job, then."

Marcus turned and walked back to his office. He closed the door, walked around to the other side of his desk, and checked his phone. Nothing. Not a single notification from Zeno. *How could he have caught Antonia and not told the rest of the Oculus?* He slumped down at his desk. *How best to play this? Should I speak to Zeno now? Should I yell and scream at him?* No, that would not play out well. He had to be cold, calculating. Maybe he should seek out the other members. Maybe he should ask them what they thought. Then an idea hit him.

Sentry, the young man who had supposedly taken out Titus, was here. What if he told Aria about that? She would go after him in her grief, or maybe she would confront Zeno herself. Either way, all he had to do was light the fuse and see how it played out. Maybe he would get lucky. Maybe Aria and Bartholomew would take each other out, and he could swoop in and take over. That would make things easier.

He smiled and headed down toward Aria's lab. Aria was typing away at her computer. He walked in acting like he was overworked and fatigued.

"My goodness," he said, wiping his brow exaggeratedly. "It's a zoo out there. Everyone is in such a buzz."

Aria looked up from her computer. "What's going on?"

Marcus started walking over to her desk. "Apparently, they caught Antonia and her agent friend, Sentry."

Immediately, Aria shot up from her computer chair, knocking it backwards. "They found her? Did they say anything about Titus?"

"I haven't heard anything at all," Marcus said, holding his hand up to his forehead as if he was thinking. "I'm not sure."

"Who authorized it?" she asked. "Was it you?"

Marcus stepped back. "No, I didn't even know about it until it was already done. Apparently, the guards brought them to speak with Zeno, so I guess he's your man."

Aria walked toward the door. Marcus turned and followed behind her, smiling all the while.

Upstairs, Sentry was still planning when there was a loud knock at the door. He looked up and saw three figures enter the room. He stood up hesitantly. An uncertain feeling overcame him. He wasn't sure if they were coming in to hurt him or if they wanted something else. He made a fist, ready for whatever assault lay before him.

But instead, he was surprised when they told him to get ready for dinner. He shook his head, unsure if he was hearing them correctly. "What?" he asked.

"Get ready for dinner," one of them repeated in a strong Dutch accent.

"Oh...all right."

One of them threw a freshly pressed suit on the bed beside him. He looked at it and then back to them. The guards didn't leave, and Sentry stood there for a moment, just staring at them. He made a motion with his hand as if to shoo them away, but they stood firm.

"Well at least turn around."

Two of them did, but one didn't. Sentry rolled his eyes and grabbed the suit. He kept his Guild shirt on, as well as the tie and pants. They had specially made by Captain Duo, which meant they were alchemically designed to be more resilient and durable. Sentry looked over his shoulder at the one guard who hadn't turned around, hoping that these guards didn't ask about it. If things went the way he was expecting, Sentry would need the protection. Then he grabbed the suit jacket and put it on. Fortunately, the two suits were both black, so it worked well.

"I'm ready," he said. "Let's get this show on the road."

The four of them stepped out into the hallway. He turned and saw Antonia stepping out as well. She was also flanked by a crew of guards. Now she was wearing a black ball gown with a slit down the left leg and long gloves that went up to her elbows. She gave a little bow to Sentry, and then she turned. Sentry held out an arm for her to take. Then he looked at the guards and said, "Well, lead the way."

Flanked on all sides, the two prisoners walked down the hall. At the end of the hallway was a huge elevator. They all entered and one of the guards punched in a button on the panel. The elevator descended. When they hit their floor, the doors opened and there were two more guards waiting for them. Two of the guards stepped out first and motioned for them to follow. Sentry and Antonia stepped out next, with four more guards in front. The rest trailed behind them in a tight formation.

They could see a lush, red carpet that led down to closed double doors. They were lavishly designed with two long handles and a bronze symbol on each door. Both of them had the same Egyptian-style eye on the door. Sentry found himself scoffing a little. It seemed a little on the nose to have such a symbol on the doors of a secret society that called themselves the Oculus.

"You guys are a little overt when it comes to the iconography, huh?" Sentry joked.

"Don't look at me. I didn't do the interior design. I barely did anything, really."

Sentry nodded. They continued down the hall to the double doors. The first two guards moved to the sides and grabbed the doors. The others positioned themselves along the walls, while two more kept walking in step with Sentry and Antonia. Then the doors were pulled open. The two guards motioned for them to enter.

"Enjoy your dinner," one of them said.

DINNER WITH THE DEVIL

Inside the room was a long dinner table. It spanned at least thirty feet with maybe ten or twelve chairs down each side and one on each end. Bartholomew sat alone at the far end. He hopped up immediately and rushed over to them like they were long lost friends. He had a drink in his hands and he stopped in front of them as if he was out of breath. Sentry wasn't sure if it was just for show, or if Zeno's advanced age really made it exhausting for him to move.

"I'm so glad you could make it," he said. "Come, come, come, please, you must have the escargot." He ushered them into the spacious room. The doors slammed closed behind them. Like before, none of the other guards came in, but Sentry was certain that Zeno wasn't leaving himself unguarded. Either guards were hidden inside this room, or they could manifest inside the room at a moment's notice. But Sentry was going to operate under the assumption that they were in the room now.

Around them, Sentry could see long hanging banners of blue and gold. Each one had an Egyptian hieroglyph that represented a different god. He could see one for Ra, Anubis, Bast, and Osiris. Then there were others with that same Egyptian eye design. Each wall had several bronze sconces, making the room glow with a warm golden light. There was enough room in here for four or maybe even five hundred people. Sentry found himself wondering if the Oculus had special events or parties here. Who knew the kinds of people that the Oculus had influence over and who they might entertain here. Senators, foreign dignitaries, important ambassadors, CEOs of businesses, lobbyists, maybe even presidents and prime ministers. A cold shiver went down Sentry's spine at the thought.

As if on cue, a soothing, familiar voice came into his head. *Sentry, we have your location. Prepare for evacuation.*

No! He almost yelled into her mind.

What?

Don't do it. We aren't ready yet.

Insight sighed. *What do you mean? You are in danger, aren't you?*

No, we're fine. Just wait for my signal and then send Rikers in to get us.

Fine, just give me the signal and we'll stand by.

Sentry turned back to Antonia, hoping that he was keeping his cool. Zeno had been showing them some sarcophaguses made of gold and lapis lazuli. *Good,* Sentry thought, *they don't seem to be paying attention to me.*

Zeno went on to hand each of them a small plate. At the center of the table was a small platter with the escargot on it. Well, at least Sentry assumed it was. He had never had the unusual dish before. Antonia and Zeno both dug in, but Sentry hesitated. He had never tasted snail eggs before, and he wasn't sure he wanted to start now.

"Please, try some," Zeno said. "I promise it isn't poisoned."

Sentry stepped back, somewhat taken aback by his humor. But Zeno was eating it as well, so he tried a bite, and it wasn't as bad as he was expecting. Then Zeno walked around to the other side of the table and sat down. He held up a hand and waved, as if calling someone in. Out of nowhere, a server appeared through a secret door, holding two trays in his hands. He was followed by others, who were also holding trays. They came and placed the dishes down around Zeno.

"Come try some." He was already starting to serve himself.

Zeno began eating as Sentry and Antonia came around to sit at the only other chairs. They sat down and the servers began offering them entrees. There was lobster and steak as well as vegetarian options. They had salads and soups, along with mashed potatoes with gravy, and slightly charred asparagus. Sentry, having not eaten much at dinner earlier, took a little bit of everything. He knew that he would need his energy for the next phase of the plan. Likewise, Antonia filled her plate.

"Ah, see, isn't this nice?" Zeno asked. "You know I never had kids. Married to the job, as it were. But I'd always wished to have something of a family. That's part of the reason I created all of this. I wanted to leave something for the next generation."

Sentry's left eyebrow rose into his hair, unsure how true any of that actually was. Antonia scoffed. "Zeno, you just wanted the power. I don't believe any of that."

"No, it's true. The Oculus is my family. The power is a nice benefit. The influence we have on the world all while remaining completely ensconced in the shadows is just part of our plan. We have had our fingers in almost every part of world affairs."

He paused for a moment, wiping his mouth with his napkin.

"We had our hands in the research and development world thanks to our friend Drake. We also had an influence over academia with Professor Alexander Pius, who you've also met. Marcus Pharis is our hand in the world of gifted business, and his influence is monumental. The Oculus has had a hand in the Protectorate with me as the director and Dexter Romulus in the headquarters. You remember him, right?"

Sentry nodded. Dexter Romulus was the one they used to call Metalborn. He was the one who had created the Shadow Agency, which Sentry had taken down months ago.

Zeno put his hand around his knife. It wasn't a threatening motion, but it could be interpreted that way. "So you see, Sentry, you've been involved in my affairs for some time now. Ever since you found yourself in Dr. Drake's experiments, you have been meddling in my business."

Once again, Bartholomew Zeno paused, this time to take a bite. As he chewed a bite of steak, he looked back up. "Do you know what Dr. Drake's experiment was? The one you interfered with six or so years ago."

Sentry shook his head.

"It was for me. He was experimenting to create an artificial body. His goal was to create a synthetic body that could house my consciousness. Those extra gifts and such were a bonus. Something that lost boy that he found would have helped with. But yes, it was to give me a new, younger body," Zeno said, looking at his old, withered hands. He balled them into fists. Although he was even older, Zeno still looked like a sixty or seventy-year-old man.

"I thought that his experiments were all for him. To create a body for him to…" Sentry paused. "I don't know, take over the world."

Zeno laughed. "No, nothing so overt. The Oculus has never wanted world domination. Too messy, and not quite feasible. But influence and manipulation. That is where we make our livelihood."

"I see. So, you influence governments, the Protectorate, and businesses. Then you get the benefits, each of your members."

"Well, there are those in our organization that benefit more than others. Some, like Aria are here to push for medical change. You don't know her, but you've met her son, Titus."

Sentry's eyes widened. He had a wild expression, like he was about to be attacked at any moment.

But Zeno didn't react. "Aria is just trying find a cure for her son's rare medical diagnosis. Granted, she has made a fortune in medical pharmaceuticals, but all of it was to create a cure for him."

Sentry nodded.

"Well, now that you know some of how we operate, who some of us are, and what we aim to achieve, what is your decision. Will you join us? Be our newest members?" Zeno asked, stabbing another bite of steak with his fork and then holding it up in the air. It wasn't a subtle gesture. Sentry picked up on exactly what he meant. Then Zeno popped the steak into his mouth and chewed.

Sentry looked over to Antonia. Although he knew what his answer would be, but he didn't quite know what hers would be. Then he looked back at Zeno. Zeno was still methodically chewing on that same piece of meat, grinding it and pulverizing it.

"I haven't changed my answer, Mr. Zeno. I know you thought holding us here to show your authority, telling us about all about your organization to impress us, and then gracing us with this dinner, all with the hope that this would change my answer. But I still refuse to work with you or your organization."

"That is a shame. I would have hoped you would see all of the good you could do with us. Imagine the impact you could have with all of our resources, compared to the limited resources you have on your own."

Sentry nodded. "That might be true. But what would it mean to gain all of this, and lose my heart?"

Zeno turned and looked at Antonia. "And what about you?"

She shook her head. "I'm not coming back."

Just then, the large doors slammed open. All of the eyes in the room turned to see the woman coming through the door. She was wearing a white lab coat with peeling off white latex gloves. She made a beeline right for Bartholomew Zeno. He stood up. "Ahhh, Aria Guerrero. Just the person who I wanted to see. I have a proposition for you."

That almost caused her to take a step back. The sneer on her face immediately changed into a more quizzical one, as her eyes turned into slits. She turned her head, but her eyes stayed locked on Zeno. "What do you mean?"

"Well, unfortunately, our friends here refuse to work with us. So, I think you should handle how we eliminate these two."

"That sounds perfect to me."

Immediately, she held out her hands and on them. A strange gas emanated from her palms and lifted up in the air. That strange gas spread and moved around Sentry and Antonia. At first, His eyes grew heavy. The room began to spin. He slammed a hand on the table to hold himself up, but it didn't help anything. Then there was nothing but darkness.

FILE #22

LIGHTS OUT

Sentry could hear noise around him before he saw anything. Two voices were speaking in the distance. Sentry shook his head and his vision started to clear. The blackness gave way to light, and he began to see his surroundings. To his left, he saw Antonia. She was sitting in some kind of mechanical chair. There were mechanical clamps keeping her in place. That made Sentry look down, and he realized he was in the same kind of chair. He shifted, but he couldn't move his arms or legs.

Just then Zeno came into view. He looked down at Sentry with a fake look of concern. "Oh no, look at you."

"Where are we?" Sentry asked, almost instinctively.

"Oh, well, let's see. How do I put this? You are going to be tortured by Aria here. She is not happy about what you did to her son."

"What?" Sentry was still groggy.

"She's going to run an experiment on you. I believe it involves a new pain medication and how much pain you can endure."

Aria came into Sentry's view. She stuck the needle into the side of his arm. He winced almost reflexively, but it didn't actually hurt. "Now this is very experimental. It might not even help with the pain. But you get to be our guinea pig."

"What…" Sentry said, finally starting to feel lucid enough to understand and speak. "Don't…"

Aria leaned in, inches from his face. "Then tell me what happened to my son."

Sentry's eyes darted to Antonia for just a moment. He knew that she was the one who had dealt the final blow that sent Titus into the sea. But he knew that if he told them, they would undoubtedly redirect their torture onto her. He had to keep her alive. In the grand scheme of things, his life wasn't worth as much as hers. If she died, then they would lose their biggest asset against the Oculus.

"We fought on the deck of the boat. He came after me, and I knocked him off of the boat."

As he lied, Antonia was shaking her head at him. Sentry could tell she was about to admit that it was her. He couldn't let her do that. He had to make sure that she didn't draw attention to herself.

"Yeah, he went flying into the sea, and then we hid. No one saw us fighting, but I knocked him and his goons into the sea."

Aria turned to a chrome medical cart and grabbed a small device and then turned back to Sentry. She clicked a button on the side, and a small electric charge sparked into life. Sentry's eyes widened as he saw the small cattle prod. She stepped toward him and struck him on the leg with the cattle prod. The jolt went up his leg, and he felt the burning followed by a numbing sensation. It was like his leg was dead for a moment. Then she hit him again on the arm. Like before, the pain was like a searing brand and then a strange tingling.

Sentry lurched forward, convulsing. Antonia shook her head at him again. He could tell she regretted not saying anything. But he shook his head at her. *Don't say anything at all.*

"You took my son from me!" Aria screamed and then stuck him again with the cattle prod. Sentry screamed as his body convulsed again. The burning sensation spread along his chest. She held the metal prod down, shocking and burning. He gripped the armrests, white-knuckling them in the pain. He grit his teeth, doing everything he could to bear the pain.

From another room, Marcus watched the events transpiring. He was drumming his fingers and tapping his foot. In frustration, he stood up and paced around. As he ran through options and scenarios, he felt himself start to panic. Instead of Zeno and Aria being at odds with each other, Zeno turned the situation around and now had her on his side. This worked against what Marcus found himself trying to do. He needed to do something to bring this back around. If he was going to unseat Zeno, he would need to do something. But what?

Then a crazy idea came to him. He turned and walked out of his office. He walked past a few guards and nodded at them as he walked into one of the more secure areas. Because of his level, he could get into almost every section of the pyramid without consequence. He then passed through the next room and looked at a doorway with a sign overhead that read: *Breaker*.

He looked around before walking into the room. His heart was racing, and his hands were sweaty. Before he took the next step, he wiped his hands on his pants. He took a few quick, deep breaths as he psyched himself up for it. Then he snapped back the pyramid's main breaker.

Once the power was off, he pulled and broke off the knob. Immediately, he jumped out of the room and calling out for help in the complete darkness. He walked along the wall, moving back toward the group of guards. He looked at them and yelled, "What is going on in here?"

The guards rushed around, looking at their systems. Inside, Marcus was hoping this was going to end with him on top. It was a gamble, but he was playing for the biggest of prizes. In his mind, the risk was worth it.

Back inside the room, Sentry thought he was passing out from the pain when everything went black, but then he blinked and realized he wasn't actually losing consciousness. The chair that was holding him in place clicked and the locks opened. He realized what had happened and then pushed out with all of the energy that he had. He couldn't see what he hit, but he heard several large objects and figures slam into the nearest wall. Then he looked around for Antonia.

"Where are you?" he called.

"Right here," she said, holding out a hand.

Sentry immediately pushed out with his telekinetic radar. He could sense where she was, and he reached out to grab her hand. He turned around to face forward and put her hand on his shoulder. "Hey, I have an idea."

"What?"

"You fire, and I'll aim."

Together, the two of them moved down toward the exit. Sentry could sense their exit. He put his hand on the doorknob and turned it. At first, he was worried that it wouldn't work, but the door wasn't locked. He heard a satisfying click, and they were off.

They found themselves in a large open hallway. Like before, he pushed his radar senses out to see if anyone was nearby and could sense people down the hall. He was about to whisper to Antonia, but he didn't get a chance.

"Who's there?" someone yelled. "Team echo-niner-niner making contact."

"What do we do?" Antonia tightened her grip on his shoulder.

Before he could even respond, the voice called out once more. Same thing. But Sentry didn't know what the call sign was, but he had to say something.

"This is team bravo three, three!"

There was a moment of silence. No one called back. Then, the guards fired on them. Two bolts of energy burned the wall near them. Fortunately, they were just as blind as he was. Antonia didn't even wait. She held up her hand and charged up a blast. The energy erupted from her hand and shot down the hallway. Unfortunately, the blast was wide, but that was to be expected. Antonia wasn't a trained fighter, and she was attacking completely blind.

"Try and fire three or four degrees to your right," Sentry whispered.

"What does that mean?"

"Ugh, okay. Just move a little to the right, and then fire again."

She did as he said and fired another powerful blast to the right. This time she amped up the power and the energy blast was at least twice as big. The wall completely melted away as well as blasting the two guards. The blast exploded into the next wall and the melted wall gave off a bit of light. They could see that the rest of the hallway was empty, so they started moving. Sentry didn't know exactly which direction they were going, but anything that was away from where they were was good.

They had moved for several minutes before they ran into some more guards. Like before they called out, but Antonia blasted at them once again. She wasn't terribly good at the aiming, but she made up for it with the sheer amount of power that she could put out. She surprised Sentry every time she fired. It was so much raw output.

Sentry couldn't believe it. He wondered if she was overdoing it. Maybe she wouldn't be able to keep it up. But they ran into a third group and then a fourth, and still she wasn't slowing down. In his experience, he'd never seen someone put out so much energy before.

After several minutes of moving around in the dark, the power was finally restored. It was almost jarring when the lights finally came back on. Sentry had to cover his face for a moment as his eyes adjusted. After a second, he could see correctly. But when he turned around, he realized that Antonia wasn't behind him. He turned around and saw her moving around a corner. He turned around and went after her.

"Antonia, where are you going?" he asked.

She didn't stop and pointed ahead. He ran up beside her and saw the large double doors ahead of them. Like before, Antonia held out her hands and a massive surge of energy destroyed the doors in front of them. The large room was full of people, running this way and that. Some in mechanic jumpsuits and others in white lab coats. Some wore guard uniforms. The guards started running for the doors, but Antonia didn't stop.

"We need to get out of here!"

But Antonia didn't listen. She just kept moving. For a moment, Sentry thought about his options. But regardless of what he wanted to do, he knew that they needed her alive. Everything revolved around her. That meant Sentry needed to keep her alive.

He rushed ahead of her and summoned a shield. He looked over his shoulder at her and smiled. "We do this together."

"All right."

"Let me know when you're ready to fire."

As they moved forward, Antonia would fire, and Sentry would shield them. Once they got to the entrance, they could see the prize inside. It was a large metallic rector. This powerful energy source was what powered all of the other Oculus bases, at least that was their hope. Everything in their plan hinged on that single fact. As long as they could take that reactor out, they could cripple, if not destroy, the Oculus's activity all over the world.

FILE #23

POWER SURGE

Smoke billowed into the air as Antonia blasted the reactor. There was another explosion as metal and machinery flew off. More guards rushed at them, but Sentry was throwing them back with his telekinetic energy. After he threw another group of guards back, he looked around. Most of the scientists were fleeing for their lives. None of them realized what Sentry was after. He felt bad for a moment. They all probably assumed their lives were in danger. But Sentry wouldn't attack defenseless people.

The large reactor was still working. The massive device wasn't dead yet. It was a spinning generator that was inside of large triangular structure. It came to a large point at the top with spiked edges that gave it domineering look. The center had a solar panel where it drew in the power, but it also had two sections on the side where the gifted-powered energy cells could be inserted.

Guards were coming in from behind. He swung around to defend Antonia as the guards rushed in through the door. He flared his telekinetic energy, causing the air to ripple around him, a slight blue color in the air. The first one came in to take a swing, but Sentry pushed back with a forceful push of energy. Then another came from the side, but he deflected that one and then countered with another attack. More came at him, but he was able to shove all of them back with a telekinetic push. Then he lined up threw another force of energy, and four of them went flying out the door. Then he adjusted and pulled the door closed.

"How close are we to having that thing down?" he asked.

"Almost!" she yelled. "It's a lot bigger than I expected."

Sentry looked up at the ceiling. He could see smoke rising up to the roof. "Can you bring the roof down on the reactor?"

She nodded. "Good idea!" She blasted up at the ceiling, destroying several of the solar panels up on the roof. Then the roof exploded, sending large pieces of metal and glass down on it. A massive metal beam snapped off and crashed down on the generator. The spinning reactor was stopped when the metal beam jammed into it, but the machinery was still trying to move. There was a large spark of energy as the different pieces started to overheat. One of the computer panels exploded. Another one was smoking. Then another piece released a cloud of smoke. The face plate cracked before the unit bent out like a metallic balloon.

"I think that did it!" Sentry yelled.

"We need to get out of here!"

"Insight, we need evac, now!" Sentry yelled out, not even realizing he wasn't calling out in his mind.

In a moment that felt like an eternity, he was worried that no one was coming. But then Rikers appeared out of a puff of mist. He grabbed the two of them by the wrists. Then they exploded into a cloud of fog and were gone. Rikers moved them all along the vents and out of the building. In a matter of seconds, they were gone.

Meanwhile, Marcus was being escorted down to the lower levels. His first thought was to try and get out of the building. This whole situation was his fault. He bet wrong, and now the Oculus was crippled. He mentally chided himself for this blunder. But he told himself not to think like that. He couldn't cry about the situation. He needed to play this right.

His phone buzzed again. It had been going off every few seconds ever since the reactor was destroyed. Different contacts, bases, and other facilities were contacting him to ask why they had no power. Some said that the couldn't complete missions or fulfill orders to their clients. There would be a massive fallout if they didn't get power back on soon. Marcus didn't reply to any of them. Not yet. He needed to speak with Zeno. Hopefully, he would know what to do.

Finally, they found Zeno, and Marcus told the guards to stay behind. He came into the room, the same one where they had been torturing Sentry only a few minutes ago. Zeno was sitting in a rolling chair. Everything else in the room looked like it had been thrown against the wall.

"Where's Aria?" Marcus asked.

"She's in the medical wing. She was hurt when Sentry threw everything across the room," Zeno said, motioning to the objects against the wall.

"My word…"

"What's the damage?" asked Zeno.

"We lost power, but then Sentry and Antonia attacked the…They attacked the reactor."

"Did they?" Zeno was unable to finish the sentence.

"Yes, it's destroyed. As is the power to every single Oculus base and facility around the globe."

"This is a huge blow," Zeno said, in an oddly cool tone. Marcus had expected more of a response. This was a massive setback, maybe one they would never recover from. "This changes everything for us. We need to plan and figure out how to handle this. What's our next step?"

"We could uh…" Marcus paused, unsure of what to say. "Well, we could revisit the Protectorate chairman position, sir."

Zeno turned and nodded. "All right. Fine, let's call for a meeting and we will try and make our bid for it. It's not the plan we wanted, but this could help us regain some footing."

Somewhere on the edge of the city, a cloud of mist was moving like lightning. After entering a ventilation system. Rikers and the two others reappeared in the safe house surrounded by the rest of the team. Immediately, Antonia rushed to the trash bin and threw up everything she had eaten.

Rikers winced as he moved toward her, trying to console her. "Sorry, that happens for some people the first time they experience the mist form."

Finally, she looked up. "That was horrible."

"Yeah, that first time is like being ripped out of your body, isn't it?" Rikers winced.

Brimstone walked over and gave Sentry a hug. Sentry hugged him back. "Thank you. I didn't think you would find me."

"It took a while, but Insight is amazing," Brimstone said, pointing over his shoulder at her. "She has been trying to track you since you took off."

Sentry nodded and hung his head. "Sorry about that. I thought that was the best option."

Insight walked past Sentry, and without even looking, said, "It probably was, given the situation." Then she went over to Antonia. "Do you want anything to drink?"

"Yes, please."

"So, what's going on?" asked Rikers.

Sentry took a deep breath. Then he looked at his team—Codex, Brimstone, Insight, Rikers, and even Antonia. "Well, it's worse than we could have hoped. Bartholomew Zeno is at the very top of the Oculus. Then someone named Marcus Pharis is involved as well."

"Marcus Pharis? He owns the largest gifted placement business in the world. They help put gifted with companies that need those powers."

"That's insane," said Brimstone.

Then Sentry went on to explain everything that happened. About Zeno's hopes to enlist him. How Aria Guerrero was involved, and that both Dexter Romulus and Alexander Pius were part of the Oculus as well.

"This goes back to our first years in college," said Insight. "This organization has been working in the shadows for that long?"

"No, they have been around way longer than that. That's just when we stumbled into them."

Sentry noticed Codex move over to his computer as he finished his story. He moved over to Codex, who seemed glued to his computer. It wasn't on, but his hand was on it, which meant only one thing. Codex was getting some sort of news from it. Hopefully it was good news.

"What's going on, Codex?" Sentry asked. Brimstone came up behind him.

He didn't answer right away. But after a moment, Codex moved his hand from the computer and looked over at them. "We have some bad news."

Sentry reflexively made his hands into fist. "What's the problem?"

"I am getting reports that there is going to be a meeting by the Protectorate. It sounds like Marcus Pharis is going to be there, which is odd. He is a private business man, but for some unannounced reason, he's going to be at the meeting," Codex said.

"That's not good," said Sentry.

"Actually, it's very good," said Insight. "This means they're desperate."

Brimstone nodded. "If they are showing themselves, that could be our chance to strike."

Sentry nodded. "All right, where is this meeting?"

Codex closed his eyes, and scanned the online reports with his mind. Then he opened them and said, "It's in Germany. It's at a brand-new building."

"What building?" Brimstone was bouncing up and down.

Insight shook her head. "I bet I can guess."

Codex closed his eyes again. "It's owned by Marcus Pharis."

Insight's hands balled into fists at her side. "We need to go now. This smells of corruption and back alley dealings to me. We need to get there now and show them what the Oculus is up to."

"She's right. We need to get moving," said Rikers. "Everyone gear up and grab your stuff and let's move out."

The team rushed off to grab whatever gear they needed. Within a matter of moments, they all returned from their rooms with a small to-go bag packed and ready to go.

FILE #24

THE CHAIRMAN

Sentry sat in the window of their safe house, staring at the building across the river. He put his suit jacket on and then adjusted the fit and tightened his tie. This suit had been through these last few days. From his home Guild base, to on the run, to Greece, then Egypt, and now back in Europe. With the battles and chases, it had been a difficult few days. But now it all came down to this. Either they exposed the Oculus and caught them, or they were caught and tried as traitors.

He turned back to look at the building. Across the thin river was the old Protectorate Headquarters. It was being gutted now. Most of the building was set for demolition in the next few days. There was something strange about seeing the old HQ looking like a rundown relic like that. It made Sentry think about life without the Protectorate. What would that mean for the world? What would happen if Zeno got ahold of the Protectorate? If he was able to manipulate it, or maybe even worse to work against it. The thought sent shivers down his spine. The power he had now was immense. But if he was inside of the Protectorate committee, making decision, giving intel, and being able to stay one step ahead, it could spell disaster for the world.

Beside the old headquarters was an even larger building that was owned by Marcus Pharis. Apparently, it was just built. It even still had a red barricade around it still with caution cape. Then he saw cars beginning to drive up to the building. A retinue of guards were coming out of the cars and standing around the building. It looked like they were preparing for the committee members of the Protectorate to arrive. The lights of the building began turning on, setting the dark night air ablaze with light.

Brimstone stood beside Sentry. "Looks like it's time to get moving."

"Let's go." Sentry stood up.

The team walked down to the waterfront. Rikers was standing there waiting for them. Sentry turned his head toward Sentry. "Are we ready?"

"Yes, we can mist form over to the other side. They are covering the building, but the waterfront is still exposed. But we should move quickly before they can cover the waterfront."

Sentry turned to the river. "Let's go, then. We're about to end this, one way or another."

They all locked arms and, in a flash, they all transformed into a misty cloud. Before they could blink, they were across the water and on the other side. They came in to land, but there were guards moving toward the water front. Instead, they went up to the adjacent building. The building next door wasn't as tall, but they could see the top floor.

The lights popped on, and they could see people walking inside. Sentry could see Madame Frey as well as some others that he assumed were the members of the Protectorate committee. Zeno was walking behind them with a bearded man—Marcus Pharis. The meeting was about to begin, and they needed to get inside to stop it. They needed to expose Zeno.

"Codex," Sentry asked, "can you get me audio of what is going on inside that meeting?"

"Give me just a moment..." Codex slightly paused. "And here you go."

Codex had hacked into the security footage of the building. He then was able to access those audio files and reroute them. He transferred the audio from inside the meeting room to their earpieces.

Marcus went to the front of the room. The small microphone wasn't entirely necessary for the size of the group. Marcus scanned the room. Jules Majors, or Captain Lightbringer, was positioned at the back. He made eye contact with her. She nodded. The room was secure.

"Welcome everyone," he said. "Today I wanted all of you to be a part of a big announcement."

"Why were we called to this building?" asked one of the committee members.

Zeno stepped up to the microphone. "Well, that is two-fold. First, I'm going to be announcing my bid for the Protectorate chairman position which the illustrious Madame Frey will be giving up at the end of the month."

Several eyes shifted over to her. She nodded. It wasn't like any of them didn't know she was stepping down. The position itself wasn't one that was held for very long, but what everyone didn't know was that she was stepping down from the Protectorate committee altogether.

"Yes, I'll be stepping down from the committee," she said. "It is time to make way for new blood in the veins of our Protectorate. We need new ideas and a fresh perspective."

A few of the committee members shifted uncomfortably. Some were nodding at her words, while others looked worried.

"I would like to throw my name in the ring to be the next chairman of the Protectorate," said Zeno.

"What are your qualifications?" asked a committee member from Japan. "You're not even a committee member, but you want to be the chairman."

"Yes," said Zeno. "I have been in the Protectorate since before some of you were even born. I have helped groom some of the best agents that our organization has ever seen. I think my qualifications speak for themselves."

Several of the committee members looked unsure. A few nodded appreciatively. Others were shaking their heads, still unconvinced that someone outside of the committee itself should be the next leader of the Protectorate. There was some whispering, which wasn't what Zeno wanted. He could tell that the group as a whole wasn't convinced. A few of them looked like they agreed, but he didn't have a majority vote. Zeno looked over to Marcus with a pleading look. Marcus would have been lying if it didn't feel good to see Zeno begging like that. It was nice to be needed, especially after his last game had failed so miserably. If this plan worked, it would give the Oculus the needed boost they needed. Without it, they were crippled. Maybe even dead.

"That is where we come to our second reason for being here," said Marcus. "This facility."

All eyes were immediately back on Marcus. "What do you mean this facility?" asked one of the committee members who represented Europe.

"It is no secret that your previous facility was attacked, and as such the Protectorate has been working out of a different building until they can update their security or find a new building. However, I have a third and maybe even better option. A brand new, state-of-the-art facility for the Protectorate. This building."

"You would be giving this entire building to the Protectorate?"

"Yes," said Marcus. "As part of a donation, and it is my endorsement of the illustrious Bartholomew Zeno."

Marcus backed away from the microphone and began clapping. Bartholomew stepped back up to the stand and looked out. At first, none of the committee members clapped. They were sharing looks, some skeptical. Others were confused. Some were even against it, standing there with their arms crossed.

"The building has an update communication system, completely ready to begin operations," said Zeno, reading from a card in his hand.

Then a few members clapped.

"Our facility has a more secure vault system, as well as, more levels for remote agents and analysts."

Then some more began clapping. With each of the new features he listed, more began to clap. More and more chimed in until almost the entire crowd of members were clapping.

"Think of the improvements we could make," said Zeno.

"We would be able to begin operations more effectively," said one members.

"We've been needing an updated communication system for some time now," said another.

"The building itself is much bigger than our old one," said a third.

Zeno added, "The possibilities are endless."

Outside, Insight looked at the others. Her eyes were wide and her jaw was tight. "He's bribing them. He is bribing the entire Protectorate."

Sentry realized what she meant. The building was a bribe, because otherwise, the Protectorate committee was not going to give him the position. But now they were all clapping. They were all but accepting his proposition. "We need to move now!"

Rikers yelled, "Grab hands!"

They all grabbed arms and they were instantly transformed into a cloud of mist. Their steam-like form moved up and into the vents on the side of the building. Then they came out into the room. In a flash, they transformed back into their human forms.

"Stop!" yelled Sentry. All eyes turned to them. "Don't do it. Don't elect Zeno as your new chairman. We have proof that he has been actively working against the Protectorate."

Insight stepped up beside him and pushed out with her mind, sharing his thoughts. As she did that, Sentry continued to explain the situation.

"Zeno is part of an organization that calls themselves the Oculus. I have seen him working against the Protectorate. He even captured me and had me tortured."

As he spoke, Insight took the images from Sentry's own mind and put those memories into each of the committee members' heads.

"You can't simply believe the allegation of this young man," said Zeno. "Besides, he is wanted by the Protectorate."

"They are wanted for something that you did," said Antonia.

"And I know you may say that you cannot be certain that these memories are real. That is why we have brought her with us," he said, pointing to Antonia. Insight and Brimstone remained in a tight formation around her with Rikers behind her.

"Who is that?" asked one of the members.

Another said, "Is that Antonia Sagas?"

"It is," said Insight. "She has proof that Bartholomew Zeno has been working against the Protectorate and has been involved in countless illegal endeavors and criminal enterprises."

Eyes turned to Bartholomew. "What is she talking about, Zeno?" someone asked.

A bald man shook his hands. "Can you explain this?"

"How does she know?"

A woman asked, "Where is your proof?"

Antonia stepped up, careful to remain close to her guards. "I know because I was a part of this group. I was forced to help them when my parents died, but they gave me the tools to bring down Zeno and the Oculus."

"Well, this changes everything," said one of the committee members.

Madame Frey stepped forward. "We will begin a full investigation. You," she said pointing to Sentry. "And you," she said pointing to Zeno. "Will be put in holding cells until we can sort all of this out."

Lightbringer saw only one path through this. She held up a hand and summoned her power. A large shard of solidified light energy shot toward Antonia. She couldn't have dodged it if she wanted to. The movement was too quick, and she never saw it coming. Unlike Insight.

Insight heard Lightbringer's thought since her mental link was still active with everyone in the room. She knew the attack was coming, and did the only thing she could do. She stepped in front of the large spike. Insight dropped to the ground. As she did, the light faded, leaving the wound now open. Red stained her suit.

FILE #25

WHERE THE LIGHT GOES

Sentry screamed, dropped to the ground, and cradled her head. "No, no, no! Please!"

Sentry, no Gabriel. In this moment, the agent was gone. He was that same college kid who had a crush on a girl. He wasn't the agent anymore. He was just a boy, who cared for this girl. And she was dying.

"Please, don't go," he cried.

She looked up at him, eyes fluttering. "I wish we had one more chance."

She coughed and blood dribbled down the side of her mouth. Looking up at Sentry, she tried to move her hand up to his cheek, but couldn't make it. It dropped to the ground. Brimstone looked around the room as the committee members were all screaming and taking cover. Lightbringer, Zeno, and Marcus were nowhere to be found.

As he moved, Brimstone called into his earpiece, "Codex, can you find Zeno, Marcus, and that assassin?"

Once again, Sentry let out a scream "No!"

A few moments later, Brimstone called out to the others, "No sign of them here. Codex, please tell me you have something for me."

"Yes, I found them. They're heading to the old building," said Codex.

"The old building? The one that's going to be torn down. Why?"

"Not sure yet, but the team needs to move. Now!"

Brimstone turned to see Sentry stand up. It was like looking at a different person. It was still Sentry, but he had changed. In that moment, Sentry looked like someone else. His eyes were red from crying, and there was a trail of tears down his face. His hair was messier than usual. As Sentry stood, he ran a hand through it, slicking it back. His mouth was set in a firm line, although there was still a slight tremble in his lips. Was that from rage or sadness? Brimstone didn't like the look of it. Sentry looked like a broken man.

Sentry made eye contact with Brimstone. "Let's get them." He turned to Madame Frey and said, "Keep Antonia safe, please."

She nodded. And in a flash, with Rikers's help, the three of them were gone. They turned to mist and passed through the vents out into the open air. Across the way, they traveled over to the other building. They could easily get to the old Protectorate building since a few windows were already broken and parts were already being prepped for its destruction. They landed up on the upper floors. Sentry couldn't tell the exact number, but they were definitely near the top.

"Codex, what's their location?" he asked.

"They're moving up. I think they have a helicopter on the top floor," said Codex. "I'm seeing two other guards with them. I would infer that one of them is a short-range teleporter."

Instantly, the three of them rushed up the stairs. They turned the corner and ran up the following one as well. Realizing they weren't making progress, Rikers grabbed Brimstone and Sentry and mist formed once again. The three of them shot up four flights in a second and reappeared up on the stairs just behind Zeno and his retinue of guards.

Brimstone threw a fireball at the first guard. It exploded on the ground behind him, and he was sent flying into the wall. The second guard went flying and fell down the stairs. Lightbringer turned and saw that they were being followed. "Go on without me!"

The others rushed on without her. Brimstone yelled, "I got—"

But Sentry cut him off. "No, she's mine."

Rikers took the situation into his hands and grabbed Brimstone. They evaporated into a puff of smoke and were able to maneuver around the stairs to cut off Zeno and Marcus. Brimstone held out his hand and a small flicker of embers licked up his hands. The embers sparked into a full flame around his fingers and into the air. "Option one, you come along quietly. Option two, I bring you in quietly but unconscious."

Marcus walked up the next step and pulled off the expensive suit jacket, taking his time to not wrinkle it. "Pardon me, it's Italian-made."

"Oh, by all means." Brimstone rolled his eyes.

Marcus rolled up his sleeves and then stepped forward.

"I was hoping you would choose option two," Brimstone said.

The two rushed at each other. Brimstone shot a fireball, but Marcus held out a hand and absorbed it. The flames raged for a moment, and then it was as if his hand consumed the flames that swirled around them. He brushed his hands together. "Oh that was toasty."

"What?" Brimstone's mouth hung open.

"What? You didn't know my gift?"

"Uh, well, uh…"

"My gift is to absorb energy. All kinds of energy."

"Well, let's see what happens when we try this!" Brimstone launched a fireball at the ceiling above Marcus. The blast exploded against the upper floor. The ceiling started to crack and break down around him. First, it was pieces of the wall and ceiling, but then pipes and support beams started crashing down on him. He lunged off the stairs. Brimstone lost him in the debris and cloud of smoke. He rushed into the smoke with Rikers on his tail.

"Rikers, can you do anything about this?"

"Not much. It's too thick for me to do anything."

A kick to the head sent Rikers back toward the stairs. He turned and saw someone rushing past him. Marcus with Zeno were making a break for it. Rikers called to Brimstone and then popped into his mist form and rushed back up the stairs to cut them off. Brimstone moved in that direction, and once he had a line of sight on it, he threw another fireball. The explosion was too far to be much use, but it caused them to turn around. Rikers appeared before them.

"Stop!"

"Not likely," said Zeno.

"Come here!" yelled Marcus, trying to grab Rikers. Rikers disappeared into a puff of air, and Marcus lost him. "Neat trick." Marcus rubbed his reddish beard. "You know what my favorite energy form to absorb is?"

"What?" Brimstone slammed both knees into Marcus's chest. That threw him into the wall and he slid to the ground. Brimstone landed and held out a hand, readying another attack. "You may have a gift that gives you an edge, but I have years of combat experience. You are going down."

Marcus gave him a smirk and stood up shakily. He nodded as if to admit defeat. But then, he turned and ran for the stairs once again. Zeno was on the ground and Marcus ran right past him, making no effort to help his colleague.

Rikers rushed over to him in his mist form and then grabbed him. Marcus turned into a cloud of mist as well and for a moment he was trapped. However, something happened. Rikers felt an odd sensation. A wave of fatigue hit him, but then it became painful. He tried to drop Marcus, but it was like he wouldn't let go. He tried to pull out of his mist form, but he couldn't. He was trapped.

If he could have screamed he would have, but then there was nothing. The mist form coalesced back into a human form, but it wasn't Rikers. It was Marcus's form that stood there. Marcus cracked his neck from left to right and then turned to Brimstone. "You know, I never told you what my favorite type of energy was to absorb."

Brimstone just looked at him, horrified. *What just happened?* He was so confused and terrified that he couldn't even respond.

"It's life energy. I can even drain the life force from a person with my gift. It's a pretty amazing sensation when you drain the life from someone. You feel powerful, invincible even. And somehow I absorbed your friend's life force when he was in his cloudy shape thing. Actually I think being in his cloud form made it easy. And look, no body to clean up."

Brimstone screamed and unleashed a massive barrage of flames, hoping to bring the floor on Marcus if he had to. The walls exploded around him and the ceiling started to come down. The stairs collapsed down on the lower floors and Marcus jumped up to grab the upper ledge. He caught the step thanks to the added boost of energy from Rikers. He pulled himself up and then rushed up the stairs.

Brimstone realized his blunder and ran after him. He jumped and threw a fireball at the ground so it would explode and give him an extra lift. He caught the step and pulled himself up on a lowered beam. Then he continued rushing after Marcus.

Meanwhile, Sentry was shielding himself from Lightbringer's attacks. She was powerful. All she had to do was hold out a hand and she could release a flurry of these shards of light that looked like broken pieces of glass. They shattered against his shield. So far, she wasn't able to get through his defenses. Although she was strong, Sentry was fueled by all of his rage. He dodged her attacks and then deflected others back at her. She had a long gash on her arm from one attack that had actually struck home.

"You're not bringing me in."

"Keep telling yourself that. You're going down!" He pulled his arm back and the wall behind her collapsed. She summoned a shield of hardened light to protect her. That gave Sentry the moment he needed to close the gap. He was on her with a spinning kick that connected with her shoulder. She fell to the side and spun out, landing on her feet. She rolled backwards and then sprinted away while throwing a few more of those light shards. Most of them flew off to the left and right, but a few were on target. Sentry deflected them easily enough as he chased after her.

This time he used his gift to pull at the ground, ripping some of the flooring up underneath her. She stumbled and tripped, but she didn't lose her footing. On his next attempt, he pulled the ground directly in front of her up. She crashed to the ground, sliding on the dust-covered floor.

Sentry pounced on her, throwing a telekinetically enhanced punch at her. She rolled to the left, and his fist smashed through the floor. He threw another, connecting with her ribs. She created a dagger-like light shard in her hand and slashed at him. He jumped back and then pushed at her with his mind. She skidded and hit the wall, cracking the sheetrock. He pushed again and again, the wall behind her breaking from the pressure. Eventually there was a human-shaped hole in the wall.

"Please, don't kill me…"

"Did you show Insight that same mercy?" he asked. "Did you think about her before you attack?"

She didn't respond. What could she say? Nothing could bring him back from that rage. He was a tornado, and she was a kite. She was caught up in the fury of his power, and she had to try and weather the storm. She looked into his eyes. They were still red from crying. Those eyes were the eyes of a broken man. A person who had gone so far only to see the one thing he cared about gone.

That was when Lightbringer realized what she had done. She had killed someone that he cared about. Someone that he loved. She had killed that agent, and now Sentry was broken. He was completely shattered over this, and now Lightbringer was going to feel his wrath. In that moment, she knew that she was done for. She had awoken a fury in this person.

FILE #26

LIMIT BREAKER

Sentry looked up at her, his eyes still burning from the tears. His teeth were bared as he pushed at her with all of his might, ready to crush her. He was ready to break every vow he'd ever made to himself and his agency.

That was his one rule. He promised himself that he would never kill as an agent. His goal was to stop those people who did wrong. But it wasn't to kill. *But she deserves it...* She had killed in cold blood. And she was an agent. No, she was a captain. She led an agency. He knew that.

Then he heard a helicopter on the roof roar to life and snapped out of it. One word came to his mind: Zeno. Sentry was standing there, contemplating killing this agent, but his real goal was on the roof. Zeno had called in a helicopter, and Sentry was risking him getting away. He had been so blinded by his rage, that he was going to let Zeno get away so he could fulfill a vengeance that would only satisfy him for a second. Then he would have to deal with that pain for weeks, months, years. Maybe his entire life.

He shook his head and looked around the room. There was a metal beam on the floor. He used his mind and slammed it into the wall, pinning her tight. He did the same with one more and jumped onto the next floor. Then he rushed up the stairs to the emergency roof exit.

Zeno was stumbling his way toward the helicopter. In all of the commotion, he must have been able to sneak his way up here. His leg was bleeding, and he walked with a pronounced limp.

Just then there was an explosion, and Marcus and Brimstone come flying through the hole onto the roof. Marcus screamed as he saw Zeno getting onto the helicopter. "How dare you leave me behind?!"

Zeno said something, but it was inaudible due to the helicopter's buzzing. But they could all see the smile on his face. He looked like someone who had just laid down a game winning hand in poker. He had been holding his cards in secret, and now he had the best hand at the table. He turned and continued walking toward the helicopter.

Marcus let out another roar of fury as he grabbed Brimstone by the neck. Sentry looked over at his friend and could see he was in pain, but then something else caught his eye. It wasn't just the hold that was hurting Brimstone, it was something more. He could see a glowing emanating from Marcus's hands. Something was wrong.

Zeno turned back and smiled as he closed the door to the helicopter. The chopper started to rise up and up into the air, but Sentry knew that he couldn't let him escape. He had to do something.

But what about Jake? He stood there with the helicopter rising to his right and his best friend in pain to his left. He was in between a rock and a hard place. What would he do?

So, he did the only thing he could do. He held up a hand and pulled at both forces. He split his attention and pulled at the helicopter, catching it with his mind. With the other part of his mind, he pulled at his friend. He pulled and pulled trying to break Marcus's grip on Brimstone. For a time, he struggled. Holding onto both was trying. If it had been one or the other, he could have done so easily. But his attention and his power being split like this made it nearly impossible.

Something was making Marcus impossibly strong. He wondered if Marcus had some kind of enhanced strength. But then it came to him. He was drawing his energy from Brimstone. Marcus was sucking the life right out of him.

That changed his priorities. Not Brimstone. Not Jake. His best friend. Sentry had lost the person that perhaps he was supposed to be with. The one he cared about for years. He would not lose anyone else today. Something in him snapped in that moment. Not the rage from before. Not the pain of loss. It wasn't exactly hope, but maybe something between hope and fear. Something like desperation. He broke past his normal limits and something otherworldly fueled him.

If he didn't get Brimstone away from Marcus, there would be nothing left of him. Sentry surged with power. Then he let up on the helicopter and focused everything on his best friend. In that moment, he pulled on Brimstone and also pushed out to hit Marcus with a telekinetic force. It slammed into his head, forcing it back, giving Sentry just the advantage he needed, and Brimstone came loose. He pulled his friend to himself and then spun around.

He then redoubled his pull on the helicopter. It had almost gotten away. It was twice as high now, and almost out of reach. He pulled, catching it as it moved out over the street now. As he pulled, he heard a groan from behind him.

He looked over his shoulder. Marcus looked like he had taken steroids. His muscles were swollen and his shirt was ripping. His skin was all red and veiny. *What in the world?* Sentry thought as Marcus started walked slowly toward him, screaming as he did. Sentry needed to get he and Brimstone out of this situation now. He pulled down on the helicopter, causing it to fall. With one last big pull toward him, he made the helicopter crash.

It hit the top of the building and started to slide. The metal blades slashed at the roof as it did, causing metal and debris to fly everywhere. Sentry turned and jumped out of the way as it came flying at them at breakneck speeds. However, Marcus wasn't quite as fast. Whether because he wasn't aware of it, or because of his swollen muscles, he wasn't very quick. The helicopter slammed into him, the metal blades still ripping and spinning. Sentry didn't see the collision, but he heard the scream.

Instead of looking back, he checked on his friend. "Are you all right?"

"Yeah, I will live." Brimstone smiled.

Brimstone snapped his fingers a few times, but nothing happened. His gift. Was his gift gone? Was it drained from him like Rikers's had? Again and again he snapped, only to produce a small spark. It was like he was back in his first year of college. Back then he couldn't create fire on his own, and he had to find other ways to do so. Finally, he'd made that breakthrough and figured it out. But now he was back to nothing. Was it all gone?

"Your gift, is it…"

He was staring at his hands. "I don't know."

"Hey, it's going to be all right," Sentry said, placing a hand on his shoulder.

"Yeah, of course. Well, uh, let's go get Zeno."

"Right."

They both stood up and walked to the helicopter. They slid the door open and pulled the old man from the crashed and broken wreckage. Brimstone started reading him his rights, but Zeno cut him off. "Yes, yes, I know the speech."

Brimstone continued, more out of spite than anything now. A few moments later, a swarm of agents and even the committee were up on the roof. They took Zeno into custody as well as Brimstone and Sentry. Lightbringer and Zeno were put inside of a large prisoner's vehicle like the one outside. That made Sentry remember something.

"Hey, you'll also want to detain an agent Allbright," he said. "He was working with Zeno."

Madame Frey nodded. "We'll be doing a full investigation. Any agent that had dealings with Zeno will be brought in for questioning."

Antonia rushed up and gave Sentry a hug. "Thank you!"

"Thank *you*. We did it. We caught Zeno and the Oculus."

Madame Frey shook her head. "Well, it will be some time before we have all of them in custody, but this is a huge step forward. I feel so foolish. We let someone like that get into our organization and manipulate us like that."

"Well, let's get to work," Sentry said.

"Before we can do that, we will need to get both of you into questioning. Especially you." She pointed to Antonia. "We will do our best to get you a deal, but I think we will do everything we can to make sure you don't get any jail time."

"I'll work with you and the Protectorate to do whatever I have to. Even if I have to go to jail for it. I just want this all behind me."

***

A few days later, Gabriel returned to his personal headquarters at the Guild. He had been through interview after interview with the Protectorate. They wanted to know every aspect of what happened to him, what he did, and where he went. Some interviewers were trying to detect if he was lying, while others were trying to work on damage control. They needed to make sure none of what Gabriel did could lead to trouble for the Protectorate. But he was finally done, and he was home. Or as close to it that he could. Today was Serena's funeral. He didn't care how long it took, but he needed to be back for this.

Jake walked out of the building when he saw Sentry coming. "How are you holding up?"

"Not great, ya know? I just feel like I'm broken. How's your gift?"

"It's getting better. Progress is slow."

"That's good."

There was an awkward silence for a moment. Finally, Jake spoke up.

"I don't know what to say, but I'm here. Even if you want to sit in silence."

"Thanks, man. I think that'll help," Gabriel said. Then he hugged his best friend.

The rest of their team came out to greet him. Hugs and handshakes were shared. Many congratulations were given for Sentry doing the impossible. Without a team, without any support, he took down one of the biggest crime syndicates they had every faced. But in the end, it all just felt hollow. Now it was time for the hardest part.

They arrived at the funeral, but Gabriel wasn't sure he could move. He stayed in the car for a minute, but he couldn't make himself get up and out of the car. Brimstone sat beside him quietly. No words, no questions. They just sat there. Gabriel turned to him, his eyes bloodshot and glassy.

Jake could see the tears in his best friend's eyes. He put a hand on Gabriel's shoulder and squeezed. "This won't be easy, Gabriel. I'm not going to lie to you and tell you it will be. But it's the right thing to do. We need to be here to say farewell."

Gabriel nodded and they stepped out. The funeral was a blur. Speeches, Bible verses, words of encouragement, but in the end, he didn't know what to do. He kept it together for the most part, but when they actually buried her, he lost it. Tears poured down like waterfalls. He remained there for an hour after everyone else left. He just couldn't leave. Something kept his feet planted there like they were trapped in cement. He cried until he felt like he couldn't cry anymore. Like there was nothing left. He looked over his shoulder and saw Jake. He was giving Gabriel some space, but he never left. Gabriel waved him over.

When Jake stood beside him, Gabriel said, "Remember when we all met? We were just a bunch of college kids. We got pulled into this world of secret agents and super villains. Now, we've become agents."

"Man, those were the days. Life seemed so much simpler then," Jake said.

"Yeah, it did. I don't think I'm going to be all right, Jake," Gabriel said.

"You will. You're too strong to let anything stop you. It won't feel like it yet. It may take a few months, or even a year or two. But you will bounce back."

"Will you be there to help me on those days that I can't do it on my own?" He fought the urge to turn away, uncomfortable with being so vulnerable.

Jake looked over at him and smiled. "Of course, Gabe. Of course I will."

EPILOGUE

The day after the funeral, Gabriel returned to the office. It seemed empty that day. Although things with Serena hadn't been good for a while, there was something familiar and comforting about her being in the Guild with him. He found himself spacing out, over and over again that day. There were no immediate missions. With everything that had happened, he thought it was best. He needed some time. Maybe he should take some personal time. He had essentially been on the clock, investigating the Oculus ever since he began at SIA, so many years ago.

But now it was over. Jake, his best friend, sat in the desk next to him. But in that moment, Gabriel might as well have been lost in the ocean. He felt so distant. His mind was off in some other place.

That was when the voice came to him.

There you are.

Gabriel almost fell out of his chair when the voice spoke.

He planted his feet on the ground and grabbed the desk. *Who is this?* He asked the voice.

It's me.

Gabriel's eyes widened. He looked around the room. No one else seemed to react. "Serena," he whispered.

Of course, it's me.

How are you talking to me?

Serena chuckled. *With my gift, of course.*

Where are you?

I'm still in the medical wing. I haven't recovered yet.

Gabriel's head cocked. *What do you mean?*

Come see Mend. He will explain.

Gabriel stood up and rushed down to the medical wing. He walked down the halls, peaking into rooms until he found Mend, the Guild's physician.

"Mend, what is going on?" he said.

Mend turned around and put down his clipboard. "Ah, I was wondering when she was going to reach out."

Gabriel's neck craned and he rolled his eyes. "You need to explain. Now."

"When I arrived on the scene of her death, I rushed her back to the Guild. We operated, because we usually do. I healed her best I could, I did what I could, but I didn't think it was enough. After a few hours, I pronounced her dead. But not long after, she spoke to me. She communicated right into my mind."

"What do you mean?" Gabriel shrugged, still not understanding.

"Serena told me that she was able to use her gift to get her body into a kind of stasis. She shut down everything in her body, to preserve herself. Somehow, she did it. When we got her here, we were able to repair the wounds, mostly, and save her."

"So, she is alive?" Gabriel grabbed his forehead. "This isn't a dream?"

"She is technically alive. But she is still recovering. She will probably be in a wheelchair for the rest of her life, and she won't be a field agent anymore."

"But she's alive?"

Mend nodded. "Would you like to see her?"

Mend walked out with Gabriel on his heels. They walked down a long corridor and down a long passageway. Finally, they stopped at a far-off room. Sentry didn't even know where they were exactly. Did the medical wing actually go this far? He wondered.

Mend opened the door with a keypad. Then he stood back and motioned for Gabriel to go in first. Gabriel gulped and walked into the room.

Inside the dark room, there was a medical bed. Gabriel's eyes were wet before he even saw her. Just the thought of seeing her again made him cry. He looked up to see the fiery red hair, her pale skin, and small wrists. He smiled. She was unusually pale. Well, she was dead, so maybe that made sense.

"Serena. It's you. It's really you."

She nodded. "It's me."

"I can't believe it. You survived that."

She smiled. "Mend says it was a one-in-a-million shot."

"You might be the most powerful gifted in the world."

He leaned down and just hugged her. For minutes or hours, Gabriel couldn't really tell. He just wanted to be in this moment. He drank in her smell, the feeling of her warmth, and the touch of her arms around him. It was all too much.

Finally, he pulled back. "I could ask you to explain exactly, but I don't think I would understand it anyway."

"Probably not. I barely understand it. I just tried the only thing I could, and I was able to make it."

He nodded."

"Honestly, if Mend didn't get there and heal the wounds, I wouldn't have made it. I was able to keep my body in something like a stasis mode to keep it from bleeding out and dying. But thanks to his healing, I made it."

Gabriel looked back and smiled at Mend. "Thank you."

Gabriel turned back to Serena and asked, "So, how long will you be in this bed?"

Serena looked down. "I don't know. But that is what I wanted to talk to you about. What comes next for me and all that."

"What do you mean?"

"I have a unique opportunity."

"You don't," Gabriel paused, looking confused. "You don't want to go back into the field, do you?"

Then a voice behind him said, "I tried to convince her to become an analyst."

Gabriel looked back to see Captain V.

Serena answered back. "No, you just wanted to get me ready to replace you."

V smiled as he hugged his girl. Although she wasn't his biological daughter, she was in all but blood. He practically raised her.

"Hey, you would be amazing at my job," he smiled.

"Maybe when I am old and gray," she said.

V made a stabbing motion to his heart. Then he smiled and looked down at her.

"I am serious," Serena smiled. "I have a unique situation. I am dead. For as long as the Protectorate and the Oculus think I am dead, that means they aren't looking for me."

"The Oculus is gone," Gabriel said.

She smiled but shook her head. "A multi-billion-dollar organization doesn't just disappear overnight, Gabriel. They have operatives, agents, and conspirators all over the world. My plan is to make sure all of them. And I mean all of them are caught and brought to justice."

"So, you want me to run the operation in the light," he started.

But Serena added, "And I will run the operation in the darkness."

Gabriel nodded. "I see. Then what?"

Serena nodded but paused for a long moment. "Well, I don't know. This could be a few years."

Gabriel nodded. "Will I see you again?"

She grabbed his hand. "Of course."

Gabriel looked down.

Serena squeezed his hand. "If this near-death experience has shown me one thing, it's that I don't get a second chance."

Gabriel smiled. "Well, I mean you kind of did."

She smiled and chuckled. "I'm serious though. I only get one shot at this. I want to take it with you."

"You sure you want to make that commitment when you are going to be going all shadow agent."

Serena nodded. She grabbed his other hand. "I will need you now, more than ever. I will need not just a partner, but a rock, an anchor. I need Gabriel."

Gabriel nodded. He pulled his hands away for a moment. Serena looked shocked and saddened. But he wasn't pulling away. Instead, he wrapped his arms around her. "I will never let you go. Not this time."

CHARACTERS

Gabriel Green
   Codename: Sentry
   Gift: Telekinesis

Serena Hammond
   Codename: Insight
   Gift: Telepathy

Jake Burns
   Codename: Brimstone
   Gift: Fire manipulation

Simon Cruz
   Codename: Codex
   Gift: Technopathy

Cadence Veil
   Codename: Nyx
   Gift: Shadow Teleportation

Jin Kenichi
   Codename: Kaze
   Gift: Hyperkinesis

Andre Vincent
   Codename: V (formerly Victory)
   Gift: Enhanced Intuition

Darla Sweet
   Codename: Zion
   Gift: Psionic (Psychic) Weapons

Georgia Winters
    Codename: Ivy
    Gift: Botanokinesis (Plant Manipulation)

Frank Stone
    Codename: Duo
    Gift: Alchemical Bonding

Aiden McKinley
    Codename: Insomnia
    Gift: Doesn't require sleep

Hue Long
    Codename: Foundry
    Gift: Metal Manipulation

DeVon Santos
    Codename: DarkSky
    Gift: Weather Manipulation

Eloy Einrich
    Codename: Ein
    Gift: Time Manipulation

Minato Kenichi
    Codename: Trei
    Gift: Hyperkinesis

Hakim Varma
    Codename: Rikers
    Gift: Air Form

Roger "Rocky" Samson
    Codename: Granite
    Gift: Terrakinesis

Check out the other books in
The Gifted World Series

Follow L. D. Valencia on Social Media:

https://www.facebook.com/ldvalenciabooks

https://www.instagram.com/l.d.valencia

https://twitter.com/thegiftedworld

ABOUT THE AUTHOR

L. D. Valencia has always loved telling stories. From playing pretend with his siblings to running Dungeons and Dragons campaigns, stories have always been his passion. It wasn't until he started his master's degree that he was convinced by a student to take his ideas to the published world.

He currently lives in the Nashville area with his lovely wife and their new son. As an educator, he hopes to inspire his students to love reading and writing. This book is a testament to that dream. Education is his goal, reading is his passion, and writing is his dream.

Made in the USA
Columbia, SC
27 October 2024

44789643R00107